A Book of Giants

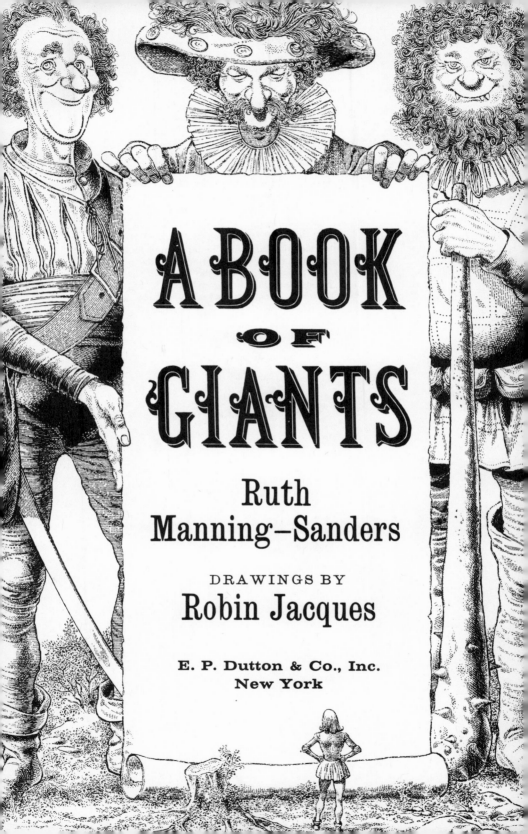

A BOOK OF GIANTS

Ruth Manning-Sanders

DRAWINGS BY
Robin Jacques

E. P. Dutton & Co., Inc.
New York

First published in the U.S.A., 1963
by E. P. Dutton & Co., Inc.

Copyright, ©, 1962 by Ruth Manning-Sanders
All rights reserved. Printed in the U.S.A.

First Printing   August 1963
Second Printing   November 1963
Third Printing   March 1964

Library of Congress Catalog Card Number: 63-15753

Foreword

The stories in this book are very old, and they come from many countries. We don't know who first told the story of *Jack and the Beanstalk*; but it has always been a favourite, and it used to be hawked about England in those little stitched-together pamphlets, called chapbooks, which travelling pedlars sold to the countryfolk for a penny or two each. The story of *The Giant and the Dwarf* comes from Georgia, the land that lies between the mountains of the Caucasus and the mountains of Armenia. *Sneezy Snatcher* comes from Cornwall, and so does *Jack the Giant Killer*. *King Johnny* was told to little Slav children in bygone days. The story of *Hans, the Horn, and the Magic Sword* comes from Jutland. *Fin M'Coul*, of course, comes from Ireland, and so do the two stories about *Conall Yellowclaw*, though these two are also told in Scotland. *The Brave Little Tailor* and *The Three Golden Hairs of the King of the Cave Giants* both come from Germany. *The Giant who had no Heart in his Body* is a Norse story, and *Prince Loaf* is a Rumanian one.

You will notice that the giants, wherever they come from, have one thing in common: they are all very stupid, and the way to overcome them is to use your wits. It is a question of 'brain against brawn'. Most of them are not such bad fellows as they are sometimes made out to be. True, they eat people when they can, but that is natural to them; and perhaps we should no more blame a giant for eating a man, than we blame a tiger for eating a deer, or a wolf for eating a sheep.

And now, we may ask ourselves, were there ever such beings as giants, outside of fairy tales? Did real live giants once exist on earth? A little while ago the answer to that question would have been 'Of course not!' But, nowadays, people are not so sure. Scientists, delving into the earth in China and Java, have come across fragments of gigantic skulls, enormous jaws, and huge teeth, which some of them think may have belonged to a race of giant men who lived on earth half a million years ago: men so big that (as the scientist, Herbert Wendt, puts it, in his book, *I looked for Adam*) they would be able to 'tear up trees by the roots, and play ball with great pieces of rock' – which is precisely what we find the giants in the fairy tales doing.

Contents

A Book of Giants

1 · Jack and the Beanstalk

Once upon a time there was a boy called Jack, who lived with his mother in a little old bit of a cottage. They had a cow, and that was all they had. They got so poor that they had scarce a morsel to eat, and no fodder for the cow.

'Jack,' said his mother one day, 'it goes to my heart to say it, but we'll have to sell the cow.'

'Why so?' said Jack.

'Hark at him!' said his mother. 'Why so, indeed? To get some money to buy us bread, you stupid lad!'

'All right,' said Jack. 'I'll drive her to market first thing in the morning. And I'll get a good price for her. I'm the boy to strike a bargain!'

So first thing in the morning Jack set out, driving the cow in front of him along the road.

It was a long way to market, and the road was hot and dusty. Jack stopped often in the shade of the hedge to rest himself, and let the cow graze on the grass by the wayside. And, whilst he was so resting, who should he see coming along the road towards him but a little odd-shaped scrap of a man with a tiny little bag on his back.

'Good-day to you, Jack,' said the little odd-shaped scrap of a man. 'And where might you be going?'

'If you know my name, I don't know yours,' said Jack. 'To market I'm going, to sell the cow.'

'I'll buy your cow, Jack,' said the little scrap of a man.

'That'll save my legs a walk, for sure,' said Jack. 'And how much will you give me?'

'More than you dream of,' said the little man.

'Ah ha!' said Jack. '*You* can't tell how much I dream of!'

The little odd-shaped scrap of a man put his tiny little bag down on the road. He opened that tiny little bag and took out five beans. 'This is what I'll give you,' said he, holding out the beans in the palm of his hand.

'Those!' said Jack. 'Five *beans* for a whole cow!'

'Five beans,' said that scrap of a man. 'But what beans! Plant them tonight, and they'll have grown to the sky by morning.'

'You don't say so!' said Jack. 'And when they've reached the sky – what then?'

'Just you go and see,' said that little odd-shaped scrap of a man.

'All right, it's a bargain,' said Jack; for he was feeling hot and tired, he didn't want to walk any farther, and he was curious about the beans.

So Jack took the beans, and the scrap of a man took the cow.

And whether he drove her north, south, east or west, or what he did with her, Jack couldn't tell. First he was on the road with her, and then he was gone, and the cow was gone.

And Jack walked home with his five beans.

'I've sold the cow, Mother,' said he. 'I got a wonderful price for her.' And he showed his mother the five beans.

He was going to tell her what marvellous beans they were, but she wouldn't listen to him. She wept and she scolded and she shouted. She held Jack's arm tight with one fist, and she clouted him over the head with the other fist. And when Jack wriggled himself free, and ran up to his garret bedroom and slammed the door, she took his precious beans off the kitchen table, where he had laid them, and flung them out of the window.

And then she sat down by the fire, and had a good cry. . . .

It was the rising sun that usually woke Jack of a summer morning, by looking in under the eaves and shining on his face. But next morning the sun did no such thing.

'Can it be raining, then?' thought Jack. And he jumped out of bed, and stuck his head out of the window.

Mercy me! What a sight! The world seemed to be wrapped in leaves! Look down, look up, look to one side or the other side, nothing could Jack see but leaves, and twisting stems: a mighty ladder of beanstalks, growing out of the earth and rising to the sky, so strong, so broad, so green, so shining, that Jack felt like a gnat must feel under the beans in a kitchen garden.

'Well,' thought Jack, 'Mother may say what she likes, but this *is* a wonderful price for an old cow! If that ladder of beanstalks doesn't reach the sky, I'm a noodle! So what next?'

Then he remembered the words of the little old odd-shaped scrap of a man, 'Just you go and see.'

'So I will then,' said Jack. And he got out of the window, and began to climb up the beanstalk.

Up and up and up and up and up! My days! It was some length of a way. But he reached the sky at last, and stepped off the highest branch of the beanstalk on to a wide, white road. Along this road he walked till he came to a very large house. And standing on the doorstep of the very large house was a very large woman.

'It's a fine morning, ma'am,' said Jack, 'and that's a fine house you live in.'

'Is it?' said the woman, staring hard at Jack.

'I had no supper last night, ma'am,' said Jack, 'nor no breakfast this morning. So I'm wondering would you be good enough to give me a bite to eat?'

'Bite!' said the woman. 'If you don't clear off good and quick, it's you will be the bite!'

'How so?' said Jack.

'Because my husband is a giant who eats boys the like of you,' said the woman. 'He's taking his morning walk just now; but when he comes back he'll have you broiled for his breakfast.'

But Jack was so hungry that he wouldn't take her warning. He begged and he prayed for just a little sup of something, till at last she felt pity for him, led him into the kitchen, and gave him some bread and cheese and milk. He had only just time to swallow it all down before he heard the giant coming, *Stamp, thump! Stamp, thump!*

'Now I'll catch it!' said the giant's wife. 'Here – into the oven with you!' And she bundled Jack into a great cold oven, and shut the door on him, just as the giant came into the kitchen.

The giant took a sniff that was like a volcano spitting. And then he roared out:

> *'Fee! Fi! Foh! Fum!*
> *I smell the blood of a Christian man!*
> *Be he alive, or be he dead,*
> *I'll grind his bones to make my bread!'*

12

'You must be ageing, I fancy, if you can't smell better than that,' said the giant's wife. ' 'Tisn't no man, at all. It's a rhinoceros I've boiled for your breakfast.'

The giant grumbled and growled for a bit. He didn't like to be told he was ageing. But he sat down at last and ate his breakfast. And, after that, he bid his wife bring him his bags of gold, and she set them on the table in front of him. Then she went out to see to their cattle. For she did all the work, and the lazy giant did nothing but eat and sleep.

He fell asleep now, with his head on the pile of gold coins he had taken out of one of the bags, and was counting. Yes, he fell asleep snoring. And Jack came quietly out of the oven.

Then Jack climbed up the table leg, and laid hold of the bag of gold that was farthest from the giant's great head, and away he went with it at a run, out of the kitchen, and through the front door, and along the wide, white road, and never stopped running till he came to the top of the beanstalk.

And then down he climbed, with the bag of gold under his arm, down and down and down and down and down, till he reached home, and gave the bag of gold to his mother.

She didn't scold him that time, nor yet did she cuff him about the head. She kissed him and called him her clever boy. And they lived on that bagful of gold till it was all spent.

Well, well, now they were poor again. And Jack's mother said poor they must remain, for she wasn't willing that Jack should meet the giant again. But Jack thought otherwise. So early one morning, when his mother wasn't looking, he climbed the beanstalk once more, up and up and up and up and up, till he reached the sky, and stepped out on to the wide, white road. And along the wide, white road he went, till he came to the giant's house, and through the front door, and into the kitchen.

And there was the giant's wife, cooking breakfast.

13

'Good morning, ma'am,' said Jack.

'Ah!' said she, stooping to glare at him. 'Where's that bag of gold?'

'I wish I knew, ma'am,' said Jack. 'It's magic the way gold vanishes.'

'Magic?' said she. 'Haven't *you* got it?'

'Why no, ma'am,' said he. 'If I had, I shouldn't be here starving for a bit of bread.'

'Well, I can believe that,' said she. 'Here!' And she gave him some bread.

Then they heard the giant coming back from his morning walk: *Stamp! thump! Stamp! thump!* So she pushed Jack into the oven and shut the door on him.

'Fee! Fi! Foh! Fum!' said the giant, and all the rest of it. And she told him again that he must be ageing if he smelt Christian men where no man was. And he didn't like to be told he was ageing, so he ate his breakfast in a sulk.

After breakfast he said, 'Wife, bring me my hen that lays the golden eggs,' and she brought the hen, and then went away to see to the cattle. And the giant said to the hen, 'Lay!' and it laid a gold egg. And he said, 'Lay!' again, and it laid another gold egg. And it went on like this till the giant got tired of the game, and fell asleep with his head on the table. And the hen pecked about on the floor.

So then Jack came out of the oven, and snatched up the hen, and away to go like the wind. But the hen cackled, and the giant's wife came running after Jack, shaking her fist and screaming. She was wearing a long apron, and she tripped over the apron and fell. And lucky that was for Jack, because he got down the beanstalk before she could pick herself up again.

'See what I've got this time, Mother!' said Jack.

He put the hen on the kitchen table and said 'Lay!' And there

14

was a gold egg. And he said 'Lay!' again. And there was another gold egg.

Now they had gold whenever they wanted it, and were rich as rich. So Jack's mother fetched an axe, and said she was going to cut down the beanstalk. But Jack said, no. It was *his* beanstalk, and he'd be blowed if he'd have it cut down. He had a plan in his head to visit the giant yet once again, but he didn't tell his mother so. *She* had a plan to cut down the beanstalk when Jack was out of the way; so she hid the axe all handy at the foot of the beanstalk, and well it was that she did so.

Jack *did* visit the giant once more. But this time he didn't go into the house and ask the giant's wife for breakfast. He feared she might wring his neck for stealing the hen and making her trip over her apron. So he hid behind a bush in the garden, till he saw her come out with a bucket and go to the pump for water. Then into the kitchen he nips, and hides himself in the flour bin.

The giant's wife came back and set about getting breakfast. And very soon after, *Stamp! thump! Stamp! thump!* in came the giant.

And didn't he sniff!

'Wife,' said he, 'I smell the blood of a Christian man! I smell him, I smell him, I *do* smell him!'

'If it's that little thief that stole our hen,' said she, 'he'll be in the oven.'

But Jack wasn't in the oven. And though they searched almost everywhere they didn't find him, because they never thought of looking in the flour bin; any more than you would, if you were looking for a boy.

'I'm vexed, wife,' said the giant, when he had eaten his breakfast. 'Bring me my golden harp to soothe me.'

So the giant's wife brought the harp and set it on the table. And then she went out to see to the cattle.

'Sing to me, harp,' said the giant.

And the harp began to sing. It sang high, and it sang low, and the sound of it was sweeter than the song of any bird.

The giant listened, and forgot he was vexed. Soon his head nodded, and his eyes closed; and there he was, sprawled over the table, asleep and snoring.

Then Jack came out of the flour bin, climbed up the table leg, snatched the harp, and away to go like the wind. But, just as he was going through the door, the harp called out, 'Master! Master!' and the giant woke up and stumbled to the door, rubbing his eyes.

When he saw Jack going like the wind down the wide white road, with the harp tucked under his arm, the giant let out a roar and pounded after him. And there they were, the two of them, Jack running for his life, and leaping like a hare, the giant roaring and taking long strides, and making the sky shake.

He'd better have saved his breath from roaring, for that slowed him up a bit, and just as he stretched out a hand to grab Jack, Jack reached the top of the beanstalk.

Then it was down and down and down and down and down, Jack scrambling for his life, but never letting go of the harp. The giant looked over the edge of the sky, took a hold of the beanstalk, and shook it. He wasn't sure if it would bear his weight. But just then the harp called out again, 'Master! Master!' and that settled it. Down and down and down and down and down the giant went climbing, and the leaves fell like rain, and the boughs groaned and bent, but they held him. So then Jack looked up, and saw the giant gaining on him.

'Mother! Mother!' shouted he. 'The axe! Bring me the axe!'

She hadn't to go looking for that axe, as you know. She picked it up from under the bottom boughs of the beanstalk, and Jack slithered the rest of the way, leapt to the ground, snatched the axe from her, and chopped the beanstalk in two. The great thing swayed this way, and it swayed that way, and then it came crashing down, and the giant came crashing down with it. He fell so heavily that he fell dead, and Jack hadn't even to finish him off with the axe.

Well now, the hen that laid the golden eggs had already made Jack and his mother rich, and the harp didn't make them any richer. But it made them more joyful. For if they were down-hearted, or tired, or sad, or if they fell out one with the other, they only had to put the harp on the table and say, 'Sing to us!' and it sang and sang, till their hearts sang with it.

They pulled down the little old bit of a cottage, and built themselves a splendid house, and it's said that Jack grew up to marry a princess. Maybe he did, and maybe he didn't. But, whomsoever he married, the harp could sing to three as well as to two, and it made no difference to Jack's mother.

2· The Giant and the Dwarf

Once upon a time a giant came to the king's palace, and banged on the gates. The gates fell down with a crash, and the giant strode into the courtyard.

'What do you want?' said the king, coming out in a hurry.

The giant was so very tall that his face seemed to be looking down at the king out of the sky. 'What do I want?' said he. 'That's easily told. I want a champion to try a bout of wrestling with me. If your champion can throw me, I'll go away, and leave you in peace. But if I prove the better man, I'll kick you off your throne, and take your kingdom for myself.'

The king, who was rather old and fat, and so couldn't think of wrestling with the giant himself, hurried in and called his knights together.

'There's a giant outside,' said he, 'and one of you will have to wrestle with him, or I shall lose my kingdom. Now, now, now, which of you is going to volunteer?'

The knights stood silent, each one trying to get behind the other. At last one of them spoke. 'We are willing to do anything in reason for your majesty. But that thing out there – it's not a man, it's a mountain. How can one wrestle with a mountain?'

'Then I shall have to lose my kingdom!' wailed the king. 'Oh, what a pity, what a pity!' And he snuffled, and shed a few tears.

Now sitting at the king's feet was a dwarf, whom the king kept to make him laugh when he was sad. And when the dwarf saw the

18

king in tears, he puffed out his little chest and said, 'You leave the giant to me. *I'll* deal with him!'

'*You!*' said the king, and he actually did laugh. 'Why, he could crush you with his little finger!'

'Not so,' said the dwarf. 'It is *I* who can twist him round *my* little finger.'

And he took a sponge full of water and a bag of flour, and out he strutted into the courtyard.

The giant was getting impatient. 'I can't wait here all day,' said he. 'Has the king chosen his champion?'

'*I* am his champion,' said the dwarf.

The giant doubled up with laughter. He laughed so loud that all the windows in the palace rattled, and a lot of the glass fell out.

'Fight first, and laugh last,' said the dwarf, 'if there's anything left of you to laugh with. But, before we fight, we'll have a trial of strength. You show me what you can do, and I'll show you what I can do. Can you squeeze any water out of a stone?'

The giant picked up a stone and squeezed it so hard between his palms that a few drops of water oozed out of it. 'See that?' said he. 'Is your head harder than this stone, midget?'

'Pooh!' said the dwarf. And he, too, picked up a stone. He squeezed the stone between his palms, and a whole stream of water ran over his hands and down on to the ground. 'Is your head harder than this stone, mountain?' said he.

The giant stared. The dwarf had the sponge in his hands, as well as the stone, and the water was running out of the sponge. But of course the giant didn't know that.

Then the giant picked up another stone and flung it on to the ground with such a crack that it crumbled to dust. 'See that?' said he. 'So will your body be when we come to wrestle, midget.'

'Pooh!' said the dwarf. He picked up a stone and flung it into

19

the air, and such a cloud of white dust fell down all round him
that he was completely hidden by it.

The giant stared harder than ever. *He* couldn't turn a stone to
dust merely by flinging it into the air! Neither could the dwarf.
He had thrown up the bag of flour, as well as the stone; but, of
course, the giant didn't know that.

'You see?' said the dwarf. 'So will *your* body be when we come
to wrestle, mountain. But I feel almost ashamed to wrestle with
such a weakling as you!'

The giant began to think he had got the worst of the bargain.
'You're the strongest little midget I ever came across!' said he.
'We won't wrestle after all. For then I should have to kill you,
and all your strength would be wasted. Tell you what – you come
home and live with me.'

'I don't mind if I do,' said the dwarf.

So the two of them set off together for the giant's house.

Outside the courtyard, the giant pulled up a tree, which he said
he would take home for firewood. He trailed the tree behind him,
and the dwarf, who couldn't keep up with his long strides, jumped
up on to the tree, and had a ride among the branches. But every
time the giant turned round, the dwarf hopped off the tree, and
began running with all his might.

'What a slow walker you are!' said he.

'Am I?' said the giant. 'Well, I suppose I have to be. If I walked
any faster, my feet would sink into the ground.'

'Then I wouldn't be in your shoes,' said the dwarf. '*My* feet
always do what I tell them.'

By and by they came to a broad, swift-flowing river. The giant
stepped into it, and the water swirled up white and foaming against
his knees.

'Come on!' said he to the dwarf.

The giant was using the tree as a staff now, to steady himself in

the water, so the dwarf couldn't ride on it any longer. But he knew that if he stepped into the river, he would be carried away by the current. So what did he do but clap his hand to his stomach, roll on the ground, and begin to yell.

'Oh, oh!' yelled he. 'This stomach ache will be the death of me! I can't come any farther. I daren't get my feet wet.'

'Well, I could carry you, I suppose,' said the giant.

'As you please,' groaned the dwarf. 'But don't you think I'd better go home?'

'No, no, I don't want you to go home,' said the giant. And he lifted the dwarf on to his shoulder, and began plunging across the river. But in the middle of the stream he suddenly stood still.

'I've been thinking,' said he. 'Strong men should be heavy; but I can't feel your weight at all.'

'Of course you can't,' said the dwarf. 'Didn't you know? I'm holding on to the sky with one hand. If I didn't do that, my weight would kill you.'

'All the same, I should like to feel your weight, just for one moment,' said the giant.

'So you shall, then,' said the dwarf. 'But I warn you, you won't like it.'

He took two big iron nails out of his pocket, and dug them with all his force into the giant's shoulder. 'I've let go of the sky,' said he. 'How does it feel?'

'Oh, oh, oh!' it was the giant's turn to yell now. 'Take hold of the sky again,' he howled, 'or I shall have to drop you!'

'I've got hold of it now,' said the dwarf. He pulled the nails out of the giant's shoulder, and the giant carried him all the way to his house.

In the giant's kitchen there was an oven as big as a barn; and in the oven there were loaves of bread as big as tables.

'Now we'll have something to eat,' said the giant. 'One of us will take the loaves out of the oven, and the other will go down to the cellar and bring up the wine. Which will you do?'

The dwarf knew he couldn't lift one of those loaves to save his life. So he said he would go down to the cellar and bring up the wine.

Down in the cellar he found a lot of huge wine jars buried up to their necks in the earth of the cellar floor. He couldn't so much as get one of those jars out of the earth, let alone carry it up the cellar steps. So he began throwing the earth about, and bumping and clattering, and making as much noise as ever he could.

'What are you doing down there?' shouted the giant.

'Just collecting the wine jars,' said the dwarf. 'I'm going to bring them all up at once, to save trouble.'

'No, no, no, you mustn't do that!' shouted the giant. 'That wine has to last me for a whole year!' And he rushed down into the cellar.

The dwarf left the giant to bring the wine, and went back up into the kitchen. He expected to find one of the hot loaves on the table by this time, but they were all still in the oven. So he took

hold of a loaf and tried to drag it out. But it was too heavy. Down
he fell on his back, and down came the hot loaf on top of him.
Try as he would, he couldn't move that great mass of bread off
his stomach, so there he had to lie.

'What *are* you doing?' said the giant, coming up from the cellar
with a wine jar on his shoulder.

'Oh, nothing much,' said the dwarf. 'I was just using one of
these hot loaves as a poultice for my stomach ache. And it's done
me a power of good. The pain's quite gone. So you can take the
poultice off, if you like.'

The giant put the loaf on the table, and they sat down to eat.

The giant was an untidy feeder. He crammed his mouth so full
of bread that some of it went the wrong way. He gave a cough and
a sneeze, and the sneeze made such a draught that the dwarf was
blown up to the ceiling. He just managed to catch hold of a beam,
and there he hung.

The giant looked up in surprise. 'What are you doing *now*?' he
spluttered.

'Be quiet!' said the dwarf sternly. 'You *sneezed*! If you do such
a vulgar thing again, I shall pull out this beam and break it over
your head.'

'I'm very sorry,' said the giant. 'I didn't know it was vulgar.
Come on down and – *A-tish-ooo!*'

He sneezed again, and the dwarf was blown off the beam and
whirled through the open window. He fell on some long grass, so
he wasn't much hurt, and he managed to pick himself up and walk
in at the door.

'This is really *too* much!' he cried. 'I can't stand such rude
manners! I'm going back to the king.'

'Oh, don't do that,' said the giant. 'I've never met a little fellow
I liked as much as you. I don't want to live alone any longer.'

'Vulgar people have to live alone,' said the dwarf. 'So I'll say good-bye. And if ever you come troubling the king again, you know what to expect. I'll fling you up in the air, and bring you down turned into dust – see if I don't!'

'I won't trouble the king again,' cried the giant. 'I promise I won't. I won't go near him. Only you stay here with me!'

But the dwarf shook his head very fiercely, and walked away. The giant stood at the door and stared after him. He felt so lonely that he wanted to cry. But he went into the kitchen and drank all the wine in the jar, and then he felt better.

It took the dwarf a long time to get home. He couldn't ford the river, so he had to go all the way round till he came to a bridge. But he reached the king's palace at last.

The king was so pleased to see him, and felt so grateful when he heard the giant was never coming back, that he built the dwarf a little palace of his own, with all the furniture just the right size for him. And he gave him a suit of cloth of gold, and a suit of cloth of silver, and another suit of green velvet, trimmed with pearls. He had little page boys to wait on him, and a little carriage drawn by the smallest of small white ponies to ride out in. He had a little wife, too, for the king wouldn't rest till he found a little lady small enough for him.

And the dwarf and his little wife lived together in splendour and contentment for the rest of their lives.

3 · Fin M'Coul and Cucullin

Some giants are stronger than others, and of all the giants that ever lived in Ireland, the giant Cucullin was the strongest. By one blow of his fist he could flatten a thunderbolt into a pancake, and he walked about the country with one such pancake in his pocket to scare the other giants. He did scare them, too. They tried to keep their distance from him, but he hunted them down, one after the other, and beat them within an inch of their lives, and then kicked them out of his road to go and nurse their wounds among the mountains.

But there was one giant whom Cucullin hadn't yet managed to kick out of his road, and that was Fin M'Coul. And the reason for that was that Fin kept out of his road so determinedly that Cucullin had never yet set eyes on him. It was through fear of Cucullin that Fin lived on the top of a windy mountain, so that he could see a long way all round him. And let Cucullin be no more than a speck in the distance, Fin would be off and hiding himself in some place or another.

Fin was only putting off the evil hour, however; for Cucullin had sworn that he would never rest by day or by night till he had met with Fin. And Fin knew they must meet. He knew it by sucking his thumb, which made things to come plain to him.

Well now, Fin was one day taking the air outside his house on the top of the windy mountain, when he chanced to put his thumb into his mouth. Then he rushed indoors to his wife, Oona, shivering and shaking.

'Cucullin is on the march this way!' said he. 'And my thumb tells me that this time I shan't escape him!'

'You and your thumb!' said Oona. 'What time is he coming?'

Fin sucked his thumb again. 'At two o'clock tomorrow,' said he. 'And do you know what he threatens to do with me? To bang me flat and carry me about in his pocket, along with his thunderbolt pancake!'

'Oh plague of my heart!' said Oona. Now Fin, my darling, you just leave this to me. Haven't I pulled you safe out of every scrape you've ever got yourself into?'

'By dad, so you have!' said Fin, and he stopped shivering and shaking.

So Oona got busy to receive Cucullin. She went down to her neighbours at the foot of the mountain, and asked each to oblige her with the loan of a gridiron. And they did oblige her, for Oona was well liked. And when she had the loan of twenty-one gridirons, she came back up home and baked twenty-four large cakes, kneading the gridirons into the middle of all but three of them. And then she set the cakes in a tidy row on a shelf, so that she should know which was which of them.

All next morning she was going to the door for a sight of Cucullin; and, sure enough, towards two o'clock she saw him far off, and small like a cloud, but getting bigger every moment. So she went in and dressed Fin up in a nightgown and a frilly cap, and brought out a huge cradle, and made him lie down in it.

'Now you are to be your own child,' said she, and she tucked a blanket round him. 'Just you lie still and say no word. Leave all to me. But you can be sucking your thumb, so you'll know if there's anything I'd have you do. . . . And by the by,' said she, as

a thought struck her, 'where does that nasty nuisance of a thunder-bolt-flattener keep his great strength?'

Fin sucked his thumb a moment, and then he said, 'In the middle finger of his right hand. Lacking that finger, there'd be no strength in him at all.'

'Be easy then,' said Oona. 'And if I'm not mistaken, here he is at the door.'

Fin shut his eyes then, and drew the blanket up round him, till there was no more to see of him than his great turn-up nose.

Oona flung the door open. And, sure enough, there stood Cucullin.

'Is this where the mighty Fin M'Coul lives?' said he.

'Indeed then it is,' said Oona. 'Come in and welcome – and sit you down.'

Cucullin sat down and looked about him. 'That's a fine child you have in the cradle, Mrs M'Coul,' said he. 'Is his daddy at home?'

'Truth then, he's not,' said Oona. 'The great bulk of him ran down the mountain some hours ago like one possessed with twenty raging devils. Seems someone told him that a little bully of a giant called Cucullin was looking for him, so he set off to catch him.

27

But pray to good my Fin won't find him, or there'll be nothing left of that poor Cucullin but mincemeat.'

'Well, Mrs M'Coul, I am Cucullin,' said he. 'And I've been looking for Fin this year or more. And though he keeps out of my way, I have taken my oath not to rest day or night, summer or winter, till I get him between my two hands.'

'*You!*' said Oona, very scornful. 'Did you ever see Fin?'

'How could I, ma'am,' said Cucullin. 'He never gives me the chance.'

'Never gives you the chance, is it?' said Oona. 'And Fin raging to make mincemeat of you! I'm thinking that the day you do set eyes on him will be your last. Take advice that's well meant, and keep out of his way. For as the wind is to the dust that flies before it, so is Fin to the likes of you. But, talking of wind now, since it's rattling the door, would you oblige me by turning the house round?'

'*Turn the house round?*' said Cucullin, quite startled. 'Is that what you're asking me?'

'Why yes,' said Oona, careless-like. 'It's what Fin does when he's at home.'

Cucullin got up and strode outside. He cracked the middle joint of the middle finger of his right hand three times. Then he took the house in his two arms, and turned it round.

And when Fin saw this, he pulled the blanket up over his eyes, and shook till the cradle rattled.

But Oona just gave Cucullin a light word of thanks, and then asked him if he would do another little favour for her.

'It's only that I'm short of water this dry weather,' said she. 'And if you'd take a pitcher and fill it for me, I'd be obliged.'

'And where shall I find the water?' said Cucullin.

'Step to the window and I'll show you,' said Oona. 'See that black rock down yonder behind the hill? There's a good spring

28

under that rock, Fin tells me. And indeed, he would have pulled the rock apart and let out the water this very morning; but the rage he fell into about you put all else out of his head. So if you'll kindly take the pitcher and see to it, I'll be able to fill the kettle and boil you some bacon. For you'll surely need something inside you to keep your strength up, if you're to escape with your life out of Fin's clutches!'

Cucullin took the pitcher and went down the mountain. He wasn't much liking all he heard tell about Fin. He stood and stared for a while at the solid black rock, that rose high as himself without flaw or seam in it. Then he cracked the middle joint of the middle finger of his right hand nine times, took the rock in his two fists, and tore it apart. He made a chasm in it four hundred feet deep, and the roaring of the water that flowed down the chasm Fin could hear in his cradle.

'Oona,' whispered he, 'I'm thinking my last hour is nigh me!'

'Wisht!' said Oona. 'No such thing, it isn't.'

And she went smiling to the door as Cucullin came back with the filled pitcher.

'Thanking you civilly,' said she. 'And now be seated and refresh yourself with a cake whilst the bacon's boiling.'

And she set before him a dozen of the cakes with the gridirons in them.

Cucullin's labours had made him hungry. He opened his mouth and took a great bite. Then he gave a yell and spat everything out. 'What sort of a cake do you call this?' he roared. 'Here's two of my best teeth gone!'

'Oh,' said Oona, 'that's Fin's special cake. He never eats any other. Nor yet does the child in the cradle. But may be 'tis a bit hard-baked for a weak little fellow the likes of you. Here – try another. This one's softer, I'm thinking.'

The cake smelt good, and Cucullin was always ravenous after

he'd been cracking his finger joint. He took a great bite; but again he yelled, and again he spat . . . and spat out two more of his teeth.

'Take your cakes away!' he spluttered. 'Before I've lost every tooth in my head!'

'Dear bless me!' said Oona. 'If you don't want the cake, you might say so quietly. *I* can't help your teeth being brittle. But you've waked the child in the cradle with your noise, and we shall have *him* yelling next!'

Fin was sucking his thumb, so he knew what Oona wished him to do. And he gave the deepest, huskiest, fullest-throated, baying roar of a yell that ever he'd given in his life.

'Thunder and lightning!' said Cucullin, all of a jump. 'What a voice he's got on him for one so young! Has his daddy a voice the like of that?'

'His daddy!' said Oona. 'When Fin gives a shout, you can hear it from here to Spain!'

Cucullin began to feel he'd perhaps been mistaken in seeking out Fin. He looked uneasily at the cradle. Fin was sucking his thumb again.

'He'll be howling for cake in a minute, see if he won't,' said Oona. 'Just when I thought to have five minutes' peace!'

'Mammy, mammy, cake! Cake, mammy, CA-AKE!' roared Fin.

'Put that in your mouth and stop your noise,' said Oona. And she gave him one of the three that had no gridirons in them.

'He'll never chew that!' said Cucullin.

But Fin gobbled it up; he was hungry as could be, and he roared for another, and gobbled that up, and roared for yet another.

But when he was half-way through his third cake, Cucullin stood up. 'I'll be leaving you now, Mrs M'Coul,' said he. 'For if the son takes after his father, I'm thinking Fin may be more than a match for me, after all.'

30

'But you'll take a look at the child before you go?' said Oona, proud, like a mother. And she whipped the blanket off Fin, who sucked his thumb, and hit the air with his other fist, and kicked with his two great legs.

'By golles, what limbs on him!' said Cucullin.

'Think so?' said Oona. 'But I'm fearing he'll not make so good a man as his daddy, after all. At that age, Fin was out fighting the wild bulls in the peat bogs.'

'You don't say so?' said Cucullin, who was wishing himself somewhere else. 'But the child must have a fine set of teeth that can eat that cake!'

'You're welcome to put your hand in his mouth and feel them,' said Oona. 'The back ones are the strongest; they're worth your feeling.'

So then Fin stopped sucking his thumb, and Cucullin put his right hand a good way back into Fin's mouth. He was feeling around when he gave a groan that could be heard in the next parish. But the groan ended in a whimper, for when he pulled his hand out of Fin's mouth, his middle finger was gone, and with it all his strength.

Oona laughed. Fin leaped out of the cradle, and threw a cake at Cucullin's head. The great flabby thing whimpered again; he was getting smaller and smaller. With the last little that was left of him he blundered out of the house, and stumbled down the mountain.

But where he fled to, none can tell. He was never more seen in those parts.

4. Sneezy Snatcher and Sammy Small

Sammy Small's mother went out to do washing for people. One day, before she went, she said, 'Sammy, be a good boy, and don't go round the corner of the street.'

'Why not?' said Sammy.

'Because, if you do, Sneezy Snatcher will have you,' said his mother.

'Who's he?' said Sammy.

'A great big giant,' said his mother.

And she pulled the heavy boots on to her feet, to keep them dry whilst she was at the wash-tub, and off she went, *Stumpetty-stump*.

Well, Sammy played round the yard for a bit, and then he got bored, and wandered out into the street.

In the street there were three little girls with a skipping-rope. Two were turning, and the third was leisurely skipping, and they were all three singing:

> 'Sneezy Snatcher,
> Boy in the pot.
> Not bad cold, but some nice hot!
> Sneezy Snatcher, I'll give 'ee warning,
> How many boys have 'ee catched this morning?'.

32

Then the two little girls twirled the rope fast as fast, and the third little girl skipped like mad, and they all began counting:

'One, two, three, four, five . . .' until the skipping girl tripped over the rope. Then one of the turning girls took her place, and she turned, and the song began all over again.

'Why, 'tis nothing but a silly girls' game,' said Sammy to himself. 'There's not such a person as Sneezy Snatcher. My mammy only said it to frighten me.'

And on to the corner of the street he marched, and round the corner he went, bold as brass.

But there *was* such a person as Sneezy Snatcher, and as he happened just then to be waiting round the corner with his sack on his back, he no sooner set eyes on Sammy than he picked him up between his finger and thumb, and dropped him, screeching and squirming, into his sack.

Away he went now to his house, which was a very big one, and into the kitchen, and there he shook Sammy out of the sack.

'Aha!' said he. 'Are you a plump boy, or are you a skinny one?'

And he began pinching Sammy's arms and legs, to feel was he fat or wasn't he; because he was so short-sighted that he couldn't tell without feeling.

'Skinny!' said he at last, very disappointed. 'We'll have to boil you.'

Then he called Mrs Sneezy Snatcher, and in she came out of the back place; and she was a great, fat giantess with a foolish-looking face.

'Dumpty, my sweetheart,' said he, 'here's a boiling boy. You keep your eye on him, while I go pluck a few herbs to put in the pot.'

'All right, Sneezy,' said she.

So off he went, and Mrs Sneezy Snatcher stood staring down

at Sammy, and Sammy sat staring up at her, and she looked so foolish that Sammy began to feel quite brave.

'Does Mr Sneezy Snatcher always have boys for dinner?' said he.

'When he can catch 'em, my lover,' says she.

'Does he only have boys?' said Sammy. 'Or does he have pudding as well?'

'Oh, pudding!' said Mrs Sneezy Snatcher. 'I do dearly love a bit of pudding, but it's not often we can rise to it. Times is bad for us poor giants.'

'My mammy made a great big pudding this very morning,' said Sammy.

'I wish I was your mammy, then!' said Mrs Sneezy Snatcher.

'A pudding as big as your head,' said Sammy.

34

'Ah-h!' sighed Mrs Sneezy Snatcher.

'With raisins and currants in it,' said Sammy.

'Don't, don't!' cried Mrs Sneezy Snatcher.

'And I know she'd give you some,' said Sammy. 'Shall I run home and ask her?'

'My days, how kind!' said Mrs Sneezy Snatcher. 'Yes, go, there's my handsome. But mind you come back in time to be boiled.'

'I'll run like the wind,' said Sammy.

And run like the wind he did. But he didn't come back to be boiled.

5 · Hans, the Horn, and the Magic Sword

Once upon a time, and far away in the north part of the world, there lived a farmer and his wife and his son, Hans. And they set out on a pilgrimage to Rome.

At night they came to a forest, and it was there they had to sleep, for they found nowhere else. So two slept, and one kept awake to watch, lest evil fall on them unaware. The father took the first watch, and Hans the second.

Now when it was Hans' turn to watch, he picked up his gun and walked here and there for a bit; and then, seeing a very high tree, he climbed to the top of it. The tree was so high that he could look over the forest into the country beyond, and the moon was shining. And, by the light of the moon, what did he see but three giants, sitting round a fire, eating their supper. They had spoons as big as the biggest shovels, and forks as big as the biggest hay-forks, and they were dipping their spoons and forks into a pot, and shovelling up gallons of broth, and forking up whole joints of meat.

Hans thought he would have some fun with the giants. So he took aim with his gun, and shot at one giant's fork just as he was putting it to his mouth; and the shot bent down the prongs of the fork, and they went into the giant's chin. So this giant blamed the one sitting next to him for putting a trick on him; and the giant sitting next to him waved his fork in the air, and said, 'No such thing, I didn't!' And, in the midst of their quarrelling, Hans took a shot at the second giant's fork, and the shot shivered it to pieces. And so they were quarrelling worse than ever. But the third giant got up and sat between them, to keep the peace. So then Hans shot at this third giant's fork, and shot it in two.

This third giant had more sense than the other two, and up he got and looked around to see where the shots were coming from. By and by he spied Hans up in the tree; so he came over, and reached up, and took him down, like a bird out of a nest.

'Let me go!' said Hans.

'Not I!' said the giant. 'But since you're such a good shot, I'll spare your life if you'll do what I tell you.'

'And what's that?' said Hans.

'Not far from here,' said the giant, 'is the castle of a king who has done us many a bad turn. And, to pay him out, we are going to carry away his daughter. We have cast a sleep on everything in the castle, except a little black dog; but him we cannot put to sleep, and if he barks they will all wake up again. If you will shoot this dog for us before he barks, I will spare your life.'

'Oh, all right,' said Hans.

So this giant took Hans up on his back, and the three giants strode off to the king's castle. Round the castle was a high rampart, and the giant threw Hans on to the top of it.

'Shoot the dog,' said he, 'and then go down to the courtyard and open the gate for us.'

'Oh, all right,' said Hans.

Hans went along the rampart, and down a lot of stone steps, and the little black dog came running out of a dark corner. But Hans gave it a little whistle and a little pat, and it jumped up on him and didn't bark, but wagged its tail, and followed him.

Well, Hans came into the courtyard, and the giants were waiting

37

outside the gate. But he didn't open the gate – not yet. He thought he would look round him first.

He found the door into the great hall standing ajar, and he went in and saw the guards lying asleep, some on benches, and some on the floor, with their weapons by their side.

On the wall hung a mighty sword, and under it a drinking horn, with a silver stopper and a silver rim, and words written on the rim:

'He who drinks the wine I hold,
To him belongs the sword above;
Then let him grasp it, brave and bold,
And with it win a maiden's love.'

Hans took the stopper out of the horn, and drank some of the wine. Then he put his hand up to the sword, and tried to take it down. But it was so heavy, he couldn't move it.

'Oh, all right,' said he. 'You don't belong to me.'

And he walked on to see what else he could see.

He opened this door and that door, and saw the king asleep, and the queen asleep, and the courtiers and the pages and the ladies-in-waiting, and the footmen and the cooks and the scullery maids, all fast asleep. And the last door he opened – there was the princess asleep in her bed, and she was more lovely than Hans had ever dreamed a maiden could be.

On a table by the bedside was a gold-embroidered handkerchief, and under the table a little pair of golden slippers.

Hans forgot the giants at the gate, and stood in a dream, looking down at the princess. Then he remembered the giants again, and thought it was time for him to go. He picked up the gold-embroidered handkerchief, tore it in two, and took half and left half; and he stooped to the little golden slippers, and he took one and left one. He put the half handkerchief and the slipper into his pocket, and went back the way he had come.

When he came to the great hall, he felt thirsty; so he took the stopper out of the drinking horn, tilted the horn back over his nose, and drank till there was not a drop of wine left. And now strength ran through him like a river, and he put up his hand to the sword and lifted it down with ease.

'Oh, all right,' said he, 'you do belong to me, after all.'

Sword in hand, he went into the courtyard; and the giants were outside the big gate, hot with impatience.

'Hurry, hurry!' said one.

'You found the dog and shot it?' said another.

'Open the gate!' said the third.

'Oh, all right,' said Hans. And he fumbled and fiddled with the great bolt, as if he had no strength to draw it back.

'It won't open,' said he.

'It must open!' said the giants.

'But it won't,' said Hans. 'You must bang it down.'

The giants wouldn't bang the gate down, because they said the noise would awaken the sleepers.

'Oh, all right,' said Hans. 'Here's a little gate near by the big one, and I can open that. You'll get through if you stoop your heads.'

So he opened this little gate, and the giants were in such a hurry that they all three made a stooping rush at the gate, and their heads came through it together. And Hans swung his mighty sword, and cut off their three heads at one blow.

He left the heads lying where they fell, and he opened the big gate and passed through it, and shut it behind him with a clang. Then he went back to his parents in the forest.

In the morning, when his parents saw the mighty sword, they were curious, and said, 'Wherever did you get *this*?'

'Oh,' said Hans, 'I strolled here and there in the night, and I found it lying about.' And that's all he told them.

And they went on their way towards Rome.

Now when Hans had clanged the big gate of the castle behind him, the little black dog rushed through the great hall barking, and all the sleepers awoke. They saw the heads of the giants, and they saw the empty drinking horn, and they saw that the mighty sword had gone from the wall.

'A hero has been and gone,' said the king, 'without reward or thanks!'

Then the princess came running out of her bedroom. She had one shoe off and one shoe on, and she was fluttering half a gold-embroidered handkerchief.

'Your hero has curious manners!' said she. But in her heart she was pleased. 'He took these things to remember me by,' thought she. And she smiled to herself.

The king sent messengers all through the kingdom, seeking for the hero who had killed the giants. But they got no news of him. So then the princess thought of a plan.

'We must build an inn here outside the castle where four roads meet,' said she. 'And we will put up a notice to say that any traveller may have three days' free entertainment in return for telling me his life story. Who knows but our hero may pass this way again, or some traveller may come who has news of him?'

So the inn was built, and it was never empty; travellers came from the north and from the south and from the east and from the west, and were thankful enough to have three days' free entertainment for telling their life story. But the hero did not come, nor any news of him.

All this time, Hans and his parents were travelling onwards towards Rome. They travelled the summer through, and into autumn, and then came the cold, dark days of early winter, and they were among high mountains. And Hans' mother reproached herself bitterly, saying, 'It was I who brought you on this wild goose chase. We shall never reach Rome. We shall perish amongst these mountains. Let us go back before it is too late!'

So they turned their faces northward, and started on the journey back.

After many and many a weary day, they came to the place where the four roads met, outside the king's castle.

'Hullo!' said Hans. 'Here's a new house built since we came this way before!'

And they all three stood and read the notice over the inn door.

'This is the place for us,' said Hans' mother. 'I am weary to death, and could do with three days' rest.'

So they went in and were given soft beds and good food, and the father and mother rejoiced. But Hans was troubled, and he hid the mighty sword under his mattress.

In the morning came the princess to hear their life stories.

'My story is soon told,' said Hans' father. 'I had a small farm up in the far north, and we worked hard, my wife and I, and we put a little money by. And one day, it came to my wife that for her soul's sake she must make a pilgrimage to Rome before she died. So we sold our stock and set out, and passed this way on our journey south a year ago, and were in hope of reaching Rome. But we came near to losing our lives amongst the snows of the great mountains; and so turned back, and are now on our journey home. That is my life story, O Princess.'

'And my life story is the same as his,' said the wife, 'except that before I was married I was a dairy maid.'

'And your life story?' said the princess to Hans.

Now Hans, of course, had recognized the princess, and he was in a terrible fright because he had stolen half her handkerchief and her golden slipper; and to steal from a princess must surely mean death. So he looked away from her bright eyes, and said, 'I have nothing to tell.'

41

'But you must tell your life story,' said the princess, 'for that is the rule of this house.'

'Oh, all right,' said Hans. 'As soon as I could walk, I drove the cows for my mother; and as soon as I could run, I caught the horses for my father; and as soon as I could hold a gun, I shot game for our dinner; and as soon as I could hold a scythe, I cut the hay; and as soon as I could handle a sickle, I cut the corn; and when my parents set out for Rome, I set out with them. And we passed by here a year ago, and now we pass by again, and we find a house where no house was. That's all *my* story.'

'Except that when we passed by here a year ago you found a sword,' said his mother.

'A sword!' said the princess. 'What sword was that?'

'Oh, a mighty sword,' said Hans' mother. 'So heavy that none but Hans can wield it.'

'And where *is* the sword?' said the princess.

Hans muttered that he had left it lying about somewhere.

But that wouldn't satisfy the princess. 'Fetch it and let me see it,' said she. And she gave Hans such a strange look that he shivered in his shoes. So he ran upstairs, and took the sword from under his mattress, and brought it to the princess.

Her eyes shone with joy when she saw it; but Hans was not looking at her, he was looking at the ground.

'Where did you find this sword?' said she.

'Oh, lying about,' said Hans.

But *that* did not satisfy the princess.

'I know this sword, and I know where you found it,' said she.

'Oh, all right,' said Hans. 'If you know, you know.'

And he turned to run from the room.

But the princess clapped her hands, and her guards hurried in. 'Hold this man, and search him,' said she.

So two held him, and a third searched his pockets. And out of

42

one pocket he pulled half a gold-embroidered handkerchief, and out of another pocket he pulled a golden slipper.

'And I suppose,' said the princess, trying not to laugh, 'that you found these "lying about" also?'

Poor Hans had no answer to that question; and still he did not look at the princess, and so he did not know with what delight she was looking at him. But when she sent for the king, and the king came, and the princess said, 'I have found him!' then at last Hans did look up. He looked the king fair in the eyes.

'Oh, all right,' said he. 'I *did* take the sword from your castle hall, and I *did* take the half handkerchief and the slipper from the princess' bedside. But I don't think you ought to hang me, because, after all, I did you more good than harm.'

'Hang you!' cried the princess, and her laugh rang out like a golden bell. 'Who talks of hanging?'

So then Hans looked at her, and what he saw in her lovely face made *him* laugh. He laughed long and joyously, for he felt that if he did not laugh, he must surely weep.

Then the king joined their hands, and they were married the very next day, and the little black dog danced on his hind legs at the wedding. And Hans' parents set out once more on their pilgrimage to Rome. But this time they went in a royal coach, with outriders and footmen and pages and maids-in-waiting; and reached Rome safely, and returned to the king's castle in time for the christening of their first grandchild.

6. Jack the Giant-Killer

(1) JACK AND THE GIANT CORMORAN

It wasn't any Jack *you* know, and it wasn't any Jack *I* know. It was Jack, the farmer's son, who lived in Cornwall a long time ago. There was a giant, too, who lived in Cornwall at that time, and his name was Cormoran.

Cormoran lived in a cave on a rocky island, and he was a hungry, *hungry*, HUNGRY giant. He ate boys and girls, and men and women, and cows and sheep and pigs and horses. He would come wading ashore, waving his spiked club, and smashing and grabbing, and snatching up this, that and the other to take back to his cave. And if he had been allowed to go on much longer, there wouldn't have been a thing left alive in those parts.

Well, one winter's day, the mayor and the councillors locked themselves in the town hall to hold a meeting, because *something* had to be done about Cormoran. One said they should do this, and another said they should do that; but they none of them knew what to do, and that was the truth of it. And whilst they were arguing, there came a great hammering at the door; but nobody would open it – they were too frightened. So then there came a great crash at the window that broke the glass, and they all jumped up and hid under the table, for they made sure it was Cormoran. But it wasn't Cormoran, it was Jack. He leaped down from the

44

window-sill, and the mayor and the councillors crawled out from under the table.

'What's the reward for killing the giant?' said Jack.

'I've heard tell there's enough treasure in his cave to make a man rich for life,' said the mayor. 'You're welcome to all of it, if you can kill him. But you must mend that window.'

'When I get my treasure, I will,' said Jack, and laughed, and jumped out of the window again.

He took a pickaxe and a shovel and a horn and some long, thin planks. As soon as it was dark, he got into a boat and rowed over to Cormoran's island, towing the planks behind him. He could hear Cormoran snoring in his cave, and it was like all the waves in the world roaring together.

45

'Sleep you sound, and sleep you well,' said Jack. 'And don't you wake up till morning!'

Cormoran didn't wake up. Why should he? He was afraid of nothing, and he liked to sleep long and soundly, especially on dark winter nights, after he'd been eating all day.

Jack worked with his pickaxe and shovel all the night long, and in front of the cave he dug a huge great pit, twenty feet deep and twenty feet broad; and he covered the pit over with the planks, and strewed the planks with seaweed. By the time the sun rose, the pit was ready; so then Jack stood on the far side of it, put the horn to his lips, and blew a rousing blast: *Tantivy! Tantivy! Tantivy-y-y!*

Cormoran leapt up, rushed to the mouth of the cave, and roared out:

> *'Who dares to rouse a giant in his wrath,*
> *That man shall be the giant's morning broth!'*

And Jack answered:

> *" 'Tis I, little Jack,*
> *With the sun at my back!*
> *But with sun in his eyes,*
> *The old giant dies!'*

'Sun or no sun, I can see you well enough,' bawled Cormoran. 'And into my breakfast pot you go!'

Yes, Cormoran could see Jack well enough, because the sun was shining on Jack's yellow hair. But he didn't see the pit covered with planks and seaweed at his feet. And as he took a step forward, with his great arm outstretched to make a grab at Jack, Jack took a leap backward. Cormoran made a rush forward then, and trod on the planks. The planks broke under him, and down he went, head over heels, into the pit.

Before he could scramble out again, Jack was at him with the pickaxe, and the pickaxe went into his head. And there he was, dead as a door-knocker.

Then Jack dug a channel and let the sea into the pit; and the dogfish and the crabs had a merry time of it, eating up old Cormoran, till there was nothing left but his bones.

Meanwhile, Jack went into the cave, and the treasure that was there you wouldn't believe – chests full of gold, and chests full of silver, and chests full of rubies and pearls. And when Jack had got all that treasure to shore, he was a rich lad indeed!

He bought his father the biggest farm in all the seven parishes, and he gave his mother a necklace of pearls and bracelets of rubies; and there weren't any poor people in that part of the country for a long time, for Jack gave money away with his right hand, and with his left hand. He became very famous and got a new title by order of the mayor and councillors; and his title was JACK THE GIANT-KILLER. They couldn't knight him, because only the king could do that, but they presented him with a sword and a belt with a rhyme on it. This was the rhyme:

> 'Here's the valiant Cornishman,
> Who slew the giant Cormoran.'

It was the mayor's daughter who embroidered these words on the belt in letters of gold.

(II) JACK AND THE GIANT TANTAREM

Jack thought he would go on his travels, and maybe kill another giant or two. So, with a light step and a merry heart, he set off walking into Wales.

Now there was a giant called Tantarem who lived in a wood on the borders of Wales, and he was a cousin of Cormoran's. And when he heard how Jack had killed Cormoran, he swore to be revenged. He was thinking of making a journey into Cornwall to find Jack and kill him, when it so happened that Jack, in his journeying, came to the outskirts of the very wood where Tantarem lived.

It was a hot day, and Jack was thirsty and sleepy, for he had walked many miles. In a little grassy dell he stopped to drink from a clear stream of water that was bubbling from a rock. And when he had drunk his fill, he stretched himself out on the grass beside the stream, and fell fast asleep.

And so it was that whilst Jack slept, the giant Tantarem came to the stream to fill his water pitchers. When he saw a man lying by the water, he stooped down to see what manner of man it was. Tantarem had only one eye, but it was a very big one, and he could see with it even in the dark, like a cat. So it didn't take him long to read the words embroidered on Jack's sword belt:

> 'Here's the valiant Cornishman,
> Who slew the giant Cormoran.'

When Tantarem read those words his eye glowed and his heart bounded, for here was his enemy at his mercy. So he let his water pitchers lie, and lifted Jack, very, very quietly, on to his shoulders, and carried him away through the wood towards his castle, thinking how he would put him in a pot and cook him for supper.

As they went through the wood, the leaves of the trees brushed against Jack's neck and woke him.

'Now I'm in a scrape, sure enough!' thought Jack. 'And 'twill take all of my wits to get me out of it!'

Looking down, he saw that the track leading to the giant's castle was strewn with human bones, and the nearer they drew to the

48

castle, the thicker lay the bones. 'And if I don't look sharp about me,' thought Jack, 'I wouldn't say but that my bones won't soon be lying amongst them!'

Tantarem carried him into his castle, and locked him up in a big room, while he went back to the stream to fetch his water pitchers. The room was over the great iron door of the castle. There were no windows, only barred gratings, but the bars were wide enough apart for Jack to stick his head through. He put his head out and looked down, then he quickly pulled his head in again. For the ground was such a long, long way down that to look at it made him feel quite giddy.

'And if I were to jump out,' thought he, 'I should never reach earth alive!'

But then, in a corner of the room, he found a long coil of thick rope.

He was just going to tie the rope to the bars and let himself down by it, when he heard Tantarem stamping back into the court-yard. 'Oh my five wits, 'tis now or never!' thought he. So what did he do? Faster than fast, he made a running noose in one end of the rope, and flung the other end over a beam with the end dangling down. Then, as Tantarem was busy turning the key in the great iron door, Jack let down his noose, and caught him neatly round the neck.

Tantarem looked up with a roar. 'What are you a-doing of now, you little small thimbleful of mischief?' he bellowed. 'That won't save 'ee!' But he was too stupid to think of lifting the noose from his neck.

So Jack skipped to the end of the rope that was dangling over the beam, took it in his two hands, hung on, and pulled with all his might. The noose round the giant's neck drew tight, and tighter, and tighter still: he spluttered, he choked, he turned black in the face. And when his tongue hung out and his one eye goggled,

49

Jack slipped through the grating, and slid down the rope, and cut off his head with his sword.

And that was the end of Tantarem.

(III) JACK AND THE WELSH GIANT

Jack walked on into Wales. The roads were twisting and narrow, and they led him on and on, through woods and over mountains, till he completely lost his way. When night came he was in a narrow valley among the hills, and there was neither house nor inn where he might sleep.

But, by and by, he saw a light ahead of him, and walking towards it he saw it was shining from the window of a monstrous huge house. Except for this one light, the house was in darkness; but he groped about till he found the door, and then he knocked on it, good and loud.

'Who's that knocking, and what will he be wanting?' came a voice from within.

It was such a roaring voice that Jack knew it must belong to a giant, but he spoke up boldly:

> ' 'Tis the valiant Cornishman,
> Who slew the giant Cormoran.
> Food and shelter does he lack –
> Open then to little Jack.'

So the giant unbolted the door. He was a terrible great giant, with two stupid-looking heads. But he was a cunning one, and he opened his two silly mouths in a wide grin, and told Jack he would be welcome.

'Whilst he sleeps we can kill him easy,' whispered one silly mouth to the other silly mouth.

And he gave Jack food, and showed him to his bedroom.

'It's pleasant dreams I will be wishing you,' said he. 'And should there come any noises in the night, don't you be scared now. 'Twill only be the dratted rats at their dancing, whatever.'

'Never fear,' said Jack, 'I shan't stay awake listening to the rats dancing.' And he yawned loudly.

But he did stay awake; for he didn't trust the sly look in that old giant's four eyes.

By and by he heard the giant walking up and down in the next room, and muttering to himself. The giant couldn't mutter softly, if he tried, and Jack could hear every word he said.

'Thinks himself a brave boy, does he? Thinks there's nothing to be scared at? Thinks the old giant has a little soft heart and wouldn't harm a mouse? Thinks he can sleep and snore and take his rest, as if he was in his bed at home?

> '*But he shan't see the morning light,*
> *My club shall dash his brains out right.*'

'We'll see about that,' said Jack to himself. And he slipped out of bed, laid a big block of wood on the pillow, and went to hide behind a cupboard.

By and by the giant opened the door, felt his way over to the bed, and brought down his spiked club, *whack, whack, whack!* on the place where Jack's head should have been.

The block of wood splintered into pieces.

'Indeed to goodness, how his bones do crack, whatever!' said the giant, and off he went, laughing.

In the morning, when Jack came down to breakfast, the giant stared with all his four eyes.

'Did you sleep well, at all?' he asked.

'Oh aye,' said Jack. 'Well enough. One of your rats ran over the pillow and gave me some flicks with his tail. But that didn't worry me very much.'

'It's a hard head you have!' said the giant. 'But we shall see what we shall see. And now we'll have some breakfast.'

He gave Jack a bowl with six gallons of porridge in it, and brought in two bowls for himself, one for each head. He had two shovels for spoons, one in each hand, and he shovelled the porridge into both his mouths at once.

'It's you is a hearty eater for your size,' said he, marvelling at the way the porridge in Jack's bowl was disappearing.

But Jack had a leather bag under his coat, and he was dropping the porridge into the bag; because he didn't want the giant to think he had a small appetite.

'I could eat that much again,' said he, when the bowl was empty. 'But first I'll show you a trick.' And he took a knife and ripped up the bag, and out came all the porridge. 'I'll wager my life you can't do that,' said he.

'Can't I, indeed?' said the silly giant.

And he took a knife and ripped up his belly; and out came all the insides of him.

So that was another giant dead.

(iv) JACK, THE KING OF ENGLAND'S SON, AND THE GIANT WITH THREE HEADS

Now it so happened, in those days, that a princess was carried off by a demon, and shut up in a castle in Wales. And when the King of England's son heard of it, he said he would set her free, and he rode off into Wales. But on his way he fell among thieves, and they took his horse, and robbed him of all he had. He was wandering about, not knowing where to go, or what to do, when he met with Jack.

The prince told Jack his story, and, said Jack, 'We'll travel on together.'

'But where shall we sleep this night?' said the prince. 'I haven't one penny to pay for a bed.'

'No matter,' said Jack. 'A mile or two from here lives a giant with three heads. I was on my way to kill him. It's in his castle we'll sleep this night. You stay here, under this bush, and I'll go and arrange it.'

The prince hid himself behind the bush in fear and trembling. He thought he had seen the last of Jack. But Jack went on his way till he came to the giant's castle, and there he knocked on the gate.

The giant put his three heads over the gate.

'Who knocks?' said the first head.

'Who knocks?' said the second head.

'Who knocks?' said the third head.

'Who knocks-knocks-knocks?' echoed the walls and the woods and the mountains.

'Only your poor cousin, Jack,' said Jack.

'Didn't know we had a cousin,' said the three heads. 'What news, poor cousin Jack?'

'Bad news, cousin,' said Jack. 'Heavy news, terrible news! The King of England's son is marching this way with an army of sixty thousand men, and he has sworn to kill you.'

'Oh, poor cousin Jack,' blubbered the giant out of his three mouths. 'What shall I do? I can manage three hundred men, a hundred to each mouth, but I can't manage more.'

'Well, if I were you, I should hide,' said Jack.

'Oh yes, poor cousin Jack, I'll certainly hide. I'll go down into my vault, and you shall lock me in. When the King of England's son arrives with his army, give him a feast, and tell him I've gone to Scotland to visit my uncle.'

So Jack locked the giant in the vault and went to fetch the prince. And they feasted together, and went to bed and slept in peace, while the giant hid in the vault and trembled.

In the morning, Jack opened the giant's treasure chest, and gave the prince as much gold as he could carry. And he went to the giant's stables, and found a good horse for the prince, and so sent him on his way. And then he went down into the vault and released the giant.

'What news now, poor cousin Jack?' said the giant. And he was still so frightened that all his three mouths were twitching.

'Brave news!' said Jack. 'The prince's army is on the march to Scotland. They opened your treasure chest, but they didn't take much. And the prince went to your stables and took away your best horse, because his own had fallen lame. But you've plenty of horses left, and plenty of treasure. So cheer up, my cousin!'

The giant cheered up. His mouths stopped twitching, and they asked Jack what reward he would choose for his kindness.

'Oh, nothing much,' said Jack. 'I saw a few old things at your bedside that take my fancy: an old cap, and an old coat, and a rusty old sword, and a pair of moth-eaten slippers.'

'Oh, poor cousin Jack,' said the giant, 'those are treasures above all my treasures! The cap will tell you all you want to know; the coat makes its wearer invisible; the sword is the sword of sharpness, it will cut in two pieces whatever you strike with it; and the shoes are the shoes of swiftness, and will take you at one bound wherever you wish to go. But there, you have saved my life, and you shall have them.'

Jack took the cap and the coat and the sword and the shoes, and said good-bye to his three-headed cousin. He thought he ought to make himself invisible and cut off the giant's three heads with the sword of sharpness; but somehow he couldn't do it. It seemed too mean.

So he put on the shoes of swiftness, and at one bound overtook the prince.

'I think we can't be far from the castle where the demon has shut up the princess,' said the prince.

'Then I'll go on ahead and announce your coming,' said Jack. And at one bound he reached the castle.

He thought to find the princess chained to a stake, or charmed into a magic sleep, or locked in a high tower, or any one of those things that captive princesses usually are. But no such thing. To his surprise he found the princess at liberty, and holding her court as if the castle belonged to her. But she *was* held captive, all the same; she was held captive by a spell the demon had put on her; a spell that had turned her kind heart cruel.

When she heard the prince was coming, she pretended to be very pleased, and said, 'We must prepare a banquet for him.' And when the prince arrived, she feasted him royally, and called him her deliverer and her true love. But, before she went to bed, she wiped her lips with a handkerchief, slipped the handkerchief into the bodice of her dress, and said, 'You must show me that handkerchief in the morning, or you will be hanged from the castle wall.'

The prince laughed. 'I shall know where to find it,' says he. But he was troubled. It didn't seem a nice remark for a lady to make to her true love.

But Jack put on his cap of knowledge, and then he understood that the princess' heart was wicked; and he knew what she meant to do.

In the middle of the night, she called her demon, and gave him the handkerchief. The demon carried it away to his den, deep under the earth. But Jack, in his coat of darkness and his shoes of swiftness, followed at his heels.

The demon put the handkerchief on a shelf and went to bed. And Jack took the handkerchief back to the prince.

In the morning, the prince showed the princess the handkerchief, and she laughed.

'I knew you would easily find it,' said she.

But that night, before she went to bed, she kissed the prince on the lips, and said she, 'Tomorrow morning you must show me the lips that I last kissed tonight, or my executioner will cut off your head.'

'I will show you my own lips,' said the prince. But, again, he felt troubled.

In the middle of the night, the princess called up her demon. She rated him soundly for being so careless about the handkerchief, though neither she nor he knew how it had been stolen from him.

'But now we have the prince in our power,' said she. And she kissed the demon on the lips, and told him to go, and not show himself again until she called him.

The demon sank down to his den; but Jack, in his coat of darkness and his shoes of swiftness, followed at his heels. And when they reached the den, he drew his sword of sharpness, cut off the demon's head, and brought it back to the prince.

And in the morning, when the prince showed the princess the head, she gave a cry of horror, and fell down in a swoon. When she recovered from her swoon, the spell had gone from her, and she was good and kind again. All the evil that had been in her heart she completely forgot. And the prince didn't remind her of it, you may be sure of that!

The prince and the princess and Jack set off for the King of England's court in a splendid coach, drawn by eight white horses. The prince and princess were married next day. The king knighted Jack, and offered to keep him at court, but Sir Jack said he would rather kill a few more giants.

So he took his leave of the King of England, and started once more on his travels.

(v) JACK AND THE GIANT THUNDERDELL

Jack travelled far and wide in his shoes of swiftness; and somewhere in mid-England he came across two giants sitting outside a cave under a hill. The giants had only one head between them, and they were holding a conversation by tossing it from one to the other, when Jack put on his coat of darkness, ran between the giants, and caught the head on the point of his sword of sharpness. The head was cleft into two pieces, and both the giants fell down dead.

'That was almost too easy,' said Jack. And he went into the cave to look for the giants' treasure.

From the cave a passage led deep into the hill. The passage twisted and turned, and Jack stumbled along in the dark, till at last he came out into a big room, where a light was burning in a stone lamp.

This was the giants' dining-room; there was a long table strewn with bones, and a stone hearth with a fire, and over the fire an iron cauldron with steam coming from it, and its lid bouncing up and down. Jack didn't stop to see what was in the cauldron, for he heard a sound of crying and groaning coming from behind a locked door. He cut the lock in two with his sword of sharpness, opened the door, and stepped into a dungeon crowded with weeping women and groaning men.

The dungeon was the giants' larder, and the men and women were intended to go one after the other into the boiling cauldron. But when Jack told them the giants were dead and they were free, their weeping and moaning turned to joy and laughter.

Jack found the giants' treasure coffers in a cellar under the dungeon, and he split them open with his sword of sharpness, and shared the treasure equally amongst the captives. Then, singing and dancing and praising Jack, they came out into the sunlight, and all went together to a nearby castle that belonged to one of the captives. And there they feasted and made merry.

The castle was entirely surrounded by a very wide and deep moat, with only a narrow drawbridge to cross the moat by. You'd think they were safe enough inside that moat; but, in the midst of their rejoicing, a messenger came leaping over the bridge with all his hair standing on end. He told them that the dead giants had a nephew called Thunderdell, and he had two heads, and was the biggest and fiercest giant in all that part of the country. Now Thunderdell was coming like a moving mountain to avenge the death of his uncles.

'Oh what shall we do?' they all cried in terror. 'We have escaped one horrible fate only to meet another!'

But Jack laughed. 'Now you shall see some sport,' said he. He took his sword of sharpness and went on to the middle of the drawbridge, and made a cut in it on either side, so that all that was firm of it was just a narrow gangway in the middle. Then he put on his coat of darkness, and went across the moat to meet Thunderdell.

There he came, the moving mountain, waving his club, and gnashing all the teeth in his two heads. He couldn't see Jack, but he could smell him, and as he came he was roaring out:

> '*Fee! Fi! Foh! Fum!*
> *I smell the blood of a Cornishman!*
> *Be he alive, or be he dead,*
> *I'll grind his bones to make my bread!*'

Jack put on his shoes of swiftness, threw off his coat of darkness, and sang out:

> '*Here's little Jack, the Cornishman,*
> *Who slew the giant Cormoran.*
> *If you can touch him, 'fore or 'hind,*
> *I give you leave his bones to grind!*'

And off he went like the wind, round and round the moat, with Thunderdell bounding after him, and making the ground shake at every step.

'I'm gone!' cried Jack (putting on his coat of darkness). 'And now you see I'm here!' (slipping off the coat again).

And round the moat, and round the moat, and round the moat they raced.

Thunderdell was puffing and roaring and beating about with his great club, out he only beat the air, for Jack kept always just out of his reach.

'I'm not tired yet,' said Jack, 'but I think you are, so we'll make an end.' And he leaped on to the drawbridge and ran lightly over it. Thunderdell clattered after him; but when he got to the middle of the bridge, where it was all but cut in two, his weight broke it down, and into the moat he tumbled. And when he waded to the side, and put up his ugly heads to try and scramble out, Jack stooped, and cut both the heads clean off with one blow of his sword of sharpness.

'I told you I'd show you some sport,' said he to the watching crowd.

And they all went back into the castle and finished their feast.

(VI) JACK, THE GIANT GALLIGANTUA, AND THE ENCHANTER

Jack was soon off on his travels again. He travelled up hill and he travelled down dale, over rough and smooth for many a mile. Towards sunset he came to a desolate land, parched and brown, with neither tree nor stream, nor any sign of life. He crossed this land, and came to a great mountain with a little, tumbledown cottage at its foot.

By the time Jack reached the cottage, it was nearly dark.

'I can travel no farther tonight,' thought he. So he knocked at the door.

The door was opened by an old, old man. His thin white hair fell to his shoulders, and his white beard reached to his knees. His hands shook, and his lips trembled, and he peered at Jack through half-blind eyes.

'Father,' said Jack, 'can a traveller have lodging for the night?'

'Willingly, my son,' said the old, old man, in his old, thin, trembly voice. 'Though a bowl of soup and a bed of straw is all I have to offer you.'

Jack stepped in and sat down by the fire, and the old, old man brought him a bowl of soup.

'It's a lonesome spot you live in,' said Jack.

'Aye, aye,' said the old, old man, 'a lonesome and a weary spot. But it was not always so. Once, and not long ago, this hovel was a palace, and I was a strong and happy man, lord over wide and fertile lands, to the east, to the west, to the south, farther than eye could see. All gone, all changed!'

'But,' said Jack, 'how can that be?'

'On the top of this mountain,' said the old, old man, 'is a many-towered castle, where live the giant Galligantua and his friend, the Enchanter. And because I would not give Galligantua my only daughter for his wife, the Enchanter snatched her away to the mountain top in a flaming chariot drawn by two fiery griffins. He changed her into a milk-white doe, and all my people he turned into birds and beasts, and he carried them up to the top of the mountain. And my lands he made a barren wilderness, and my palace he turned into a hovel, and he struck me down in the pride of my manhood so that I became what you see now. Would he had killed me! For whilst I live I nurse the crazy hope that my daughter will one day be rescued.'

'Father,' said Jack, '*I* will rescue her!'

62

The old, old man shook his head. 'Ah no, my son, you cannot. Many and many a brave knight has tried and failed.'

'Father,' said Jack, 'do you see what is written on my sword belt?'

'I am all but blind,' said the old, old man; 'how should I see?'

Jack took off his belt and held it close to the old man's eyes. The old man peered and blinked, and made out the words:

> ' 'Tis the valiant Cornishman,
> Who slew the giant Cormoran.'

'He who can slay one giant can slay another,' said Jack.

But still the old, old man shook his head.

'What can you do, my son? The two terrible fiery griffins sit one on each side of the castle gate. They wait, and watch, and never sleep. He who ventures to pass them goes to his death. They tear all to pieces with their beaks and claws.'

'Not so,' said Jack. 'Here in my bundle I have a cap of knowledge, shoes of swiftness, a coat of darkness, and a sword of sharpness. With my shoes of swiftness I will reach the mountain top in one bound; in my coat of darkness I will walk between the griffins unseen. With my sword of sharpness I will cut off their heads. And with my cap of knowledge I am a match for an Enchanter.'

'Now heaven be praised, who has sent us such a deliverer!' cried the old, old man. And he shed tears of joy.

He spread straw on the ground, and Jack lay down and slept soundly.

Early in the morning Jack rose, put on his cap of knowledge, his coat of darkness, and his shoes of swiftness; and promising the old, old man he should soon see him again, he took his sword of sharpness, and set out on his adventure.

With one bound he reached the top of the mountain. With

another skip he was up at the top of a flight of stone steps that led to the gate of the many-towered castle. There, on either side of the gate, stood the griffins. Their watching eyes blazed like red-hot coals, their beaks shot out flames, their claws were like razors, the feathers of their wings were sharp swords, and they had iron spikes on their lashing tails. But Jack passed between them unseen; and when he had passed, he drew his sword of sharpness, and *snick, snack!* off rolled their heads.

And so he came to the castle gate.

There was a horn hanging by a silver chain on the gate, and under it were some magic words written in blood-red letters. Thanks to his cap of knowledge, Jack could read those words:

> '*He who once this horn dares blow*
> *Shall the giant overthrow.*
> *Who blows it twice shall make to fall*
> *Gates and towers, roof and wall.*
> *Who blows it thrice, in that same hour*
> *He breaks the dread enchanter's power.*'

'Ho, ho!' says Jack. 'Now we shall see things happen!'

He took down the horn, set it to his lips, and blew a mighty blast. The giant put his head out of a window. Jack waved his sword of sharpness, and *snick, snack!* off rolled the giant's head.

Jack put the horn to his lips again, and blew *two* mighty blasts. There was a roaring and a rumbling, the stones were cracking, the walls were swaying, the towers were bending. *Crash!* down fell the castle, and there was the Enchanter, with his bat's wings and his steeple-crowned hat, dancing and screaming among the ruins.

Jack put the horn to his lips yet again, and blew *three* mighty blasts. The Enchanter set himself alight, and flew up into the air, blazing and screaming. But by and by the blaze went out, and

there was nothing left but the scream. And that, too, soon faded.

Then, from amongst the ruins, and up from the clefts of the mountain, flocks of birds and a multitude of beasts of all sorts came flying and running, led by a milk-white doe. The mountain itself began to sink slowly into the earth, and, when it had disappeared, Jack found himself standing in front of a fine palace, amongst a crowd of people. Looking round him, he saw no wilderness, but a wide and fertile land of meadows and orchards and farmsteads, with men and women working in the fields and moving in and out of the houses.

Then out from the palace stepped a handsome, smiling man, with curly black hair and a short black beard; and a beautiful young girl ran from amongst the crowd, and flung her arms round his neck.

'My father! my father!' she cried.

And all the people rubbed their eyes and said, 'Surely we have been dreaming! We are come home again, and this is our noble lord the Duke, and this his lovely daughter!'

And what happened next? Why, Jack married the Duke's daughter, of course, and lived happily ever after. He killed a lot more giants, too; so that, by the end of his life, there was only one giant left in England. And that was the three-headed one that Jack hadn't the heart to kill. But that giant, too, died in the end, of old age.

7. King Johnny

There was once a widow who had three sons. Two of them were smart lads, but the youngest was a simpleton. And, because his mother felt sorry for him and petted him, his two smart brothers mocked him and called him King Johnny.

But Johnny didn't mind, he liked being called a king; it made him feel grand.

Now there came a time when there was no work to be had in that place, and the eldest brother said, 'Mother, if we stay here we shall starve. We had better go out into the world and seek our fortunes.'

'That's a good idea!' said King Johnny. 'When shall we start?'

'*You*, my poor boy!' said his mother. 'No, no, your brothers shall go, and may God go with them; but you must stay home with me.'

So she put all the food she had in the house into two sacks. And the two elder boys set out, each with his sack of food and a stout cudgel.

They hadn't been gone ten minutes when King Johnny got up from his seat by the fire, and went to the door.

'Where are you going?' said his mother.

'Out into the world, to seek my fortune with my brothers,' said he.

'My poor silly lad!' said his mother. 'What would *you* do out in the world?'

'I'm a king, aren't I?' said Johnny. 'Now I am going to find my
kingdom.'

His mother argued and scolded and pleaded and wept. But
Johnny was determined, and at last she had to let him go. He
took no food with him, because there was none left, but he travelled
all the lighter without a heavy sack on his back; and, in the
midst of a forest, he caught up with his brothers. They were sitting under a tree, eating some of the food from their sacks, and
they weren't at all pleased to see King Johnny. They told him to
go back home and when Johnny said no, he was going with them,
they said he would have to go hungry, as they had no food to
spare.

So King Johnny picked some berries to eat, and drank from a

little stream, and when his brothers got up to go on, he trailed along behind them, whistling and singing to himself.

By and by they came to a clearing, and in the clearing was a huge castle.

'Ah ha!' said King Johnny. 'This is *my* castle, I believe!'

'What nonsense have you got into your fool's head now?' said the eldest brother. 'This castle must belong to some mighty king.'

'And am I not a mighty king?' asked Johnny.

The eldest brother gave him a cut with his cudgel, and the second brother said, 'No harm in asking if they can give us work.' And he went up and knocked at the great door.

'Don't you know I never lock my doors?' said King Johnny. And he pushed the door open, and stepped inside.

His brothers expected to see him flung out, head over heels; but nothing happened, except that by and by he put his head round the door and told them to come in.

'Who says we may?' they asked.

'*I* do,' said King Johnny.

They were a bit scared, but they went in, and found themselves in a marble hall, so big that they felt like specks of dust in it. Far away at the end of the hall was a golden door, and when Johnny had opened this door, and they all went through, there they were in another great hall, and it was piled from floor to ceiling with gold coins.

'Help yourselves,' said King Johnny, with a wave of his hand. 'I think it's all mine.'

His brothers didn't stop to think whose it was; they emptied the food out of their sacks and were down on their knees in a flash, filling up the sacks with gold. And when the sacks were full, they hurried, as fast as their heavy loads would let them, out of the castle.

By this time Johnny was feeling hungry, so he lingered behind to eat up the food that the others had thrown down. Then out he went after his brothers.

'What a time you've been!' said the eldest brother. 'And we're both starving! Go back at once and fetch the food we left.'

'I can't do that,' said Johnny, 'because I've eaten it.'

The brothers were furious. They flew at Johnny with their cudgels and beat him till he fell down. Then they kicked him and cursed him, and told him to get out of their sight; and so left him crying bitterly, and went off home. Being now very rich, they built themselves a grand house and lived like lords, and took their mother to be their housekeeper.

Johnny cried himself to sleep under a tree. But when he woke up, he remembered he was a king, and went back to his castle and his hall full of gold. There didn't seem to be any one else in the castle, and though he shouted and knocked, nobody came.

'How lonely it is!' said he. 'I don't think I want to stay here all by myself. I'll go on a bit farther, and find a princess to be my wife. Then I shall have someone to talk to. And as for you,' said he to the gold coins, 'you're not doing much good piled up here. So I'll take one or two of you along, to buy me food by the way.'

He was stooping to pick up a coin or two, when he heard a most tremendous noise. The floor shook, and the walls shuddered, and in came two enormous giants.

'Thief!' shouted the first giant, picking up Johnny in his great hand.

'Squash him!' shouted the second giant.

'Put me down!' said King Johnny. 'Why should you squash me? What good will that do you? I thought this was *my* castle. But if it's yours, and you don't want visitors, you shouldn't leave your doors unlocked.'

'Well, well,' said the first giant, who wasn't a bad sort, really. 'I don't wish to be hasty. There's something in what you say.'

70

'You seem very brave for your size,' said the second giant, who wasn't a bad sort either. 'If we don't squash you, will you stay here, and guard our treasure for us?'

'I don't mind if I do,' said Johnny. 'But will there be anything to eat?'

The first giant took a little table out of his ear, unfolded it, and set it on the ground. 'When you are hungry,' said he, 'you have only to rap on this table, and say, "The dinner of an emperor!" and you will get all the food you want. Now we must be off on our travels again.'

And away they both stamped.

For a little while Johnny was quite happy. He looked into all the rooms, he climbed up into all the big chairs, and he slept in one huge bed after another, to see which was the most comfortable. When he felt hungry, he rapped on his little table, and said, 'The dinner of an emperor!' And the table at once spread itself with delicious things to eat and drink. But the giants didn't come back; nobody came, not even a thief, and Johnny began to feel lonely.

'What's the good of guarding a treasure that nobody comes to steal?' said he. 'I shan't stay here any longer.' And he tucked the table under his arm, and away he went.

He came out of the forest on to a high road, and there he saw an old hermit sitting under the hedge. He had a cornet slung over his shoulder, and he was moaning and groaning to himself.

'What are you groaning for?' said Johnny.

'Food!' moaned the hermit. 'Give me food! I'm starving!'

'Certainly you shall have food,' said King Johnny. He set down the table in front of the hermit, rapped on it, and called out, 'The dinner of an emperor!'

Immediately the table spread itself with steaming dishes and choice wines.

'Help yourself,' said King Johnny.

The old hermit had his mouth full already. He ate and ate till he could eat no more, and then he said, 'Oh day and night, but I could do with this table! Will you give it me, if I give you something more precious in exchange?'

'What will you give me?' said Johnny.

'See this cornet?' said the hermit. 'You have only to blow on it, and it will pour out armed men for you until you tell it to stop.'

'Certainly a king should have an army,' said Johnny. And he gave the hermit the table, and took the cornet in exchange.

'Now when I find my kingdom, I will set my army to guard it,' said he. And off he went, singing and whistling, along the road.

By and by he began to feel hungry. 'Oh my little table,' thought he, 'you and I should never have parted!' So what did he do but blow on the cornet. And out of that cornet armed knights came tumbling, and not only knights but horses; and each knight, as he came out, leaped on his horse and waved his sword and shouted 'Hurrah!'

'That's enough for the present,' said King Johnny.

Then the captain rode up to Johnny, and saluted, and said, 'What is your will, my lord?'

'I'm hungry,' said Johnny. 'Have you any food?'

'Alas, no, my lord,' said the captain.

'Then ride back along the road till you see an old hermit sitting under the hedge with a table,' said Johnny. 'Take the table from him, and bring it to me.'

The captain saluted, the knights galloped off; and in less than no time came galloping back with the table.

'Thank you,' said King Johnny. 'Dismiss!'

And the knights and the horses went back into the cornet.

Johnny was delighted with himself. He rapped on the table and had a good meal. And then, with the cornet slung on his back, and the table under his arm, he walked on, singing and whistling.

He hadn't gone far when he saw another old hermit. He was sitting under the hedge with a sack by his side. And he, too, was moaning and groaning.

'Hullo!' said Johnny. 'I suppose you're hungry, too?'

'Starving!' cried the old hermit. 'Some food, for pity's sake!'

'Certainly you shall have some food,' said King Johnny. And he set down the table, rapped on it, and gave the hermit the dinner of an emperor.

The hermit ate till he could eat no more. And then he asked Johnny if he would give him the table in exchange for the sack.

'You have only to put your hand in the sack,' said he, 'and you can pull out a castle, or two castles, or three, or as many castles as you fancy.'

'Certainly a king should have a castle or two,' said Johnny, and he gave the hermit the table and took the sack in exchange.

He walked quite a long way; but, in the end, of course he felt hungry again.

'Oh my little table, my little table!' said he. 'Why did I part with you? I may be a king, and I may have an army, and I may have as many castles as I want, but, all the same, I have nothing to eat, and by and by I shall starve!'

So what did he do, but call his armed knights out of the cornet, and send them to get his table back from the second hermit.

Now he had his table and his cornet and his sack, and he journeyed on merrily enough. Towards nightfall he came to an inn, and as he had a piece of the giants' gold in his pocket, he went inside and asked for a bed.

The landlord asked what he should get for his supper.

'Supper!' said King Johnny. 'You needn't get *me* any supper. But I'll give you and your wife such a supper as you've never had in all your life.' And he rapped on the table, and the three of them sat down to the supper of an emperor.

'But you must promise not to tell anyone about my table,' said Johnny. 'Somebody might take a fancy to it, you know, and steal it from me. And then where should I be?'

Of course they promised not to tell. But if the landlord didn't tell, and his wife didn't tell – then who did tell? *Somebody* told; because by next morning the news of Johnny's wonderful table was all over the kingdom, and the king heard of it.

'I should like to have the loan of that table!' said the king, smacking his lips, for he was very greedy. And he sent his chamberlain to ask Johnny if he might borrow the table for three days.

'Certainly one king should oblige another,' said Johnny.

And the chamberlain went off with the table.

Then the greedy old king amused himself by rapping on the table, and gobbling and gobbling. 'I could go on eating food like

74

this all my life!' said he. At the end of the three days he sent to ask if Johnny would sell the table. But Johnny wouldn't.

'I can't send it back, and I won't send it back,' thought the king; 'there's not a cook in my kingdom can produce such dishes.' And he had a copy of the table made, and sent his chamberlain with the copy to Johnny, and kept Johnny's table for himself.

'Now you and I will have a dinner worth eating!' said Johnny to the chamberlain. And he rapped, and ordered the dinner of an emperor.

But of course nothing happened.

'Didn't you hear what I said?' cried Johnny, rapping harder. 'The dinner of an emperor!'

Nothing happened.

'The dinner of an emperor!' bawled Johnny, banging on the table.

Still nothing happened.

So then Johnny knew that the king had tricked him. And he threw the table at the chamberlain's head.

'Tell the king that if he doesn't send back my table, I'll come with an army to fetch it!' said he.

'Pooh!' said the king, when he got the message. 'A peasant lad! What sort of an army does he think *he's* got? An army of fleas?'

And he chuckled, and sat down to the supper of an emperor.

But he didn't chuckle next morning when he looked out of the window and saw his palace surrounded by twenty thousand armed knights. No, he didn't chuckle at all! He didn't even stop to dress, but ran out in his nightgown, with a white handkerchief tied to his sceptre in one hand, and Johnny's table in the other.

'Take your table,' said he. 'I'm a wicked, greedy old man! But spare my life, and you shall marry my daughter.'

'She mayn't want to marry me,' said Johnny.

'Oh she will, I know she will!' cried the king.

And the princess did, for she liked the look of Johnny.

So they were married, and Johnny put his hand in his sack, and pulled out a very grand castle for them to live in. And very soon the greedy old king gave up his kingdom to Johnny, in exchange for being allowed to eat at the magic table.

Now Johnny was king indeed, and the princess was queen; and as she was wise, it didn't matter that Johnny was a bit simple, because he always did what she told him. King Johnny sent for his mother to live with them, and made her a duchess, and gave her a gold coronet sparkling with jewels. But she didn't wear it very often, because it was rather heavy.

For a time all went merrily. But one day King Johnny heard a great uproar in the streets, and sent a page to inquire what was the matter. The page came back to say that two strange old men had arrived, and were going about the town telling everyone that their good King Johnny was a swindler and a thief.

'Bring them to me,' said King Johnny, very much surprised.

And when they were brought, who should they be but the two old hermits

'I gave you my cornet in exchange for the table,' said the first hermit, 'and you sent armed men to take the table from me. And what is that but swindling?'

'I gave you my sack in exchange for the table,' said the second hermit, 'and you took the table back again by force. And what is that but thieving?'

'I never thought of it before,' said King Johnny. 'But I see you're right. I'll give you your cornet and your sack again.'

But they didn't want the cornet or the sack, they both wanted the table.

'But there's only one table, you can't both have it,' said King Johnny.

'Give *me* the table, I had it first!' shrieked one.

'No, give it to *me*, I had it last!' shrieked the other.

'I feel very upset,' said King Johnny. 'I don't know what to do.' And he sent for the queen. 'I don't want to be a swindler and a thief,' he said to her, 'but the table can't go to both of them.'

'No,' said the queen, 'but they can both come to the table. They must live in the castle and eat with us.'

And that's what happened. The two hermits ate at the table, which had this about it, that it stretched itself to suit the number that sat at it. The hermits sat one on each side of King Johnny, and he dressed them in fine robes, and made one his chamberlain and the other his chancellor. And though they didn't do much work, they sealed a lot of papers with two big seals King Johnny gave them. And that kept them very happy.

But King Johnny wasn't very happy. He had been called a swindler and a thief, and he remembered how he had gone off with the giants' table, without if you please, or by your leave. And his conscience troubled him.

'Well then, go and ask the giants if they want it back,' said the queen.

So off rode King Johnny on a fine great horse, and found the giants at home. He told them he was sorry he'd taken their table without permission. And would they like it back?

The giants laughed, and said they didn't want it back; they didn't like that sort of food.

'But we should very much like to eat your enemies for you,' said the first giant.

'We could begin with your two brothers,' said the second giant.

'Eat my brothers!' said King Johnny. 'What an idea! Certainly you shan't! And I haven't any enemies, so you can't eat anyone in *my* kingdom.'

77

'Then we must go and live somewhere else,' said the giants.

So they packed up and went to another country, and took their treasure with them.

And King Johnny rode back to his castle, and reigned over his kingdom long and happily. And all his people loved him.

8· Conall Yellowclaw

Conall Yellowclaw had three sons, and they played with the sons of the king of Erin. From playing they got to quarrelling, and from quarrelling to fighting with their fists, and in the fighting the eldest son of the king of Erin fell backwards, and hit his head against a stone, and lay dead.

In his rage and grief the king of Erin was for stringing up Conall Yellowclaw and his three sons all in a row. But those about the court cried, 'Shame!' It was but an accident, they said, and it might have been one of Conall's sons that fell, though it happened to be the king of Erin's. So then the king said he would spare the lives of Conall Yellowclaw and his three sons if they would bring him the brown horse of the king of Lochlann.

Conall and his three sons journeyed to Lochlann; but when they got there they did not know how to come at the king's brown horse. So Conall went to the king's miller and told him how he must have the brown horse, or he and his sons would hang.

'The king will not part with that horse for pity nor for gold,' said the miller. 'And if you are to have him, you must steal him.'

'I am thinking the same,' said Conall. 'And I am thinking that you might put me and my sons into four sacks of bran.'

So the miller put the four of them into four sacks of bran, and he and his servants carried the sacks into the king of Lochlann's stable.

Conall's three sons were for laying hands on the brown horse then and there, but Conall whispered, 'No. First we must make us four holes under the boards, and then, should any man hear us, we can creep in and hide.'

So they made hiding holes for themselves, and then they went to lay hands on the brown horse.

But the brown horse stamped and reared, and let out neigh after neigh. And the king of Lochlann heard the neighing, and said to the grooms, 'Something is troubling my brown horse. Go and see.'

The grooms went to see. But Conall Yellowclaw and his three sons had crept into their hiding holes, and the horse was quiet again. So the grooms went back to the king of Lochlann, and said, 'There is nothing troubling the brown horse.'

The same thing happened again.

Conall Yellowclaw and his three sons came out of their hiding holes, and tried to lay hands on the brown horse; and it stamped and reared and neighed, and the king of Lochlann sent his grooms to see what was troubling it.

When the grooms went to the stable, the horse was quiet again; and they looked here and they looked there, but found nothing wrong. And they went back and told the king so.

The same thing happened a third time.

And when the king of Lochlann heard the noise the horse was making, he said to the grooms, 'Something *is* troubling my brown horse, and if you cannot find out what it is, I must go myself and see.'

So the king of Lochlann went to the stable, and Conall Yellowclaw and his three sons had crept back into their holes, and the horse was quiet.

But the king of Lochlann saw the tracks of men's feet on the dust of the floor, and he followed the tracks of those feet to the hiding holes, and called his grooms, and they dragged out Conall and his three sons.

'Oh, Conall Yellowclaw,' said the king of Lochlann, 'is it you that my eyes are seeing? Is it you that have the name of a man of honour, and now I find to be a thief?'

'A thief I am,' said Conall, 'and sorrow it is for me to say it; but a thief I must be, if I am to save the lives of my three sons.'

And he told the king of Lochlann how it had all chanced.

'Conall Yellowclaw,' said the king of Lochlann, 'you need not go back to Erin, you and your three sons, to be hanged. I'm thinking I will string you all up here; for such is the judgment we pass upon thieves in Lochlann. Now you see the hard case you are in, and were you ever in a harder?'

'Yes, once I was,' said Conall.

'I should like to hear about that,' said the king of Lochlann. 'And if you can prove to me that you were ever in a harder case, or nearer to death than you are now, I will spare your lives for the sake of the telling.'

Then the king of Lochlann brought Conall Yellowclaw and his three sons into his hall, that Conall might tell his story. And the king of Lochlann's mother was in the hall, and she sat by the fire and tended it.

So Conall began his story.

'It was when I was a young man,' said he, 'and I went out to hunt. I came down to a creek of the sea, in a place I was never in before, and there I saw a boat fastened by a rope. The boat was piled up with treasure of all kinds, and I stepped into her to see what it might mean. And the next thing I knew, the boat had untied herself and was in the deep of the sea. She kept on going till she came to an island, and there I stepped out of her, and she went back the way she had come.

'I walked around wondering what I should do next, and I came to a glen, and there I saw a woman sitting, with a naked child in her lap, and a knife in her hand. She put the knife to the neck of the child, and the child laughed up at her, and she drew the knife away, and burst out crying.

'So I went up to her, and said, "What are you doing, and why do you cry?"

' "Oh," said she, "there is a giant lives here, and nought will he have, but that I must kill my child, and boil him. And I cannot do it!"

' "Where does the giant live?" said I. "Bring me to his castle, and maybe I can help you."

'So we went to the giant's castle, and there was the cauldron heating over the fire to boil the child in. We were looking at the cauldron, when we heard the footsteps of the giant.

' "Oh, what shall I do?" she cried.

' "Hide the child," said I, and she hid it under some straw; and I took a leap, jumped into the cauldron, and drew the lid down over me, just as the giant came in. The water was too hot to be pleasant, but not yet boiling.

' "Have you boiled that child for me?" said the giant.

' "He's not done yet," said the woman. And I cried out of the cauldron in a little shrill voice, "Mammy, I'm burning! I'm burning, Mammy!"

' "Ha! Ha! Ho!" the giant roared out a great laugh, and he picked up a pile of wood and thrust it under the cauldron, to make the water boil quicker.

'The water got hotter and hotter. As long as I could, I kept calling in that little shrill voice, "Mammy, I'm burning! I'm burning, Mammy!" to let the woman know I was still alive. But by and by it was burning I *was*, and my voice would speak nothing but groans. I was near my end – nearer by an hour than I am now, O king of Lochlann – when the giant fell asleep.

82

'The woman leaned over the cauldron then, and whispered, "Are you yet alive?" And I gasped out, "I am yet alive." And she lifted the lid off the cauldron and dragged me out. But I left the skirt of my coat, and the skin of my legs and thighs behind me.

'Now it came upon me that if I did not kill the giant whilst he slept, it was all over for me and for the woman and the child. So I went softly and took away his spear, without waking him; and I drove the spear through the one great eye of his that was set in the middle of his forehead. And so I killed him.

'The woman picked up the child, and we made our way to the shore – I dragging myself for pain and weakness. The boat came across for us, without our asking, and took us back to the creek where I had first seen it. And the woman and the child went one way, and I went another.

'That was the time, O king of Lochlann, when I was in the cauldron, that I found myself nearer death and in a worse case than I am now. For the water was boiling about me, and though I am to hang, the rope is not yet round my neck; and when it comes to ways of dying, I think that death by boiling would be worse than death by hanging.'

The king of Lochlann's mother, that was sitting by the fire, took the bellows and blew up the peat, and turned to look at Conall Yellowclaw by the blaze of it.

'Was it yourself that was there?' said she.

'Who else?' said Conall.

'And it was myself that was there, too,' said she. 'I was that woman, and the king of Lochlann is the child whose life you saved. And now, my son,' said she to the king of Lochlann, 'you see how it is that you must spare the life of him who saved yours, and you must spare the lives of his three sons also.'

'Conall Yellowclaw,' said the king of Lochlann, 'I owe you my life, and the life of my mother. So now the brown horse is yours, and he shall bear on his back two sacks full of treasure, and you shall give him to the king of Erin. But the treasure you shall keep for yourself.'

So Conall Yellowclaw and his three sons went back rejoicing to Erin. And Conall took the treasure to his own house, and gave the brown horse to the king.

And the king of Erin forgave Conall's three sons for the death of his own son, and held Conall Yellowclaw in high honour ever after.

9 · The Giant in the Cave

I will tell you another story, said Conall Yellowclaw, about when I was young and went out hunting. It was on the edge of the sea, I was, among cliffs and heather, chasing a hare. I lost the hare, and I looked around and saw smoke coming up between two clefts of rock. So I went to the place to see why smoke should be there, and the ground gave under me, and I fell down, and I fell farther down, till I was on the floor of a cave. But I fell on sand, and none the worse, except for bruises.

I was going to the mouth of the cave to see my way home again, when I heard a loud sound and a little sound coming towards me. The little sound was the patter of hoofs, and the loud sound was the tramping of a giant's feet. I was for hiding myself then, but could find no handy place in my hurry.

I was behind a cauldron that hung over a fire at the back of the cave, when the giant came in, driving before him four and twenty nanny-goats, with a great shaggy monster of a billy-goat leading them.

So nothing could I do but crouch behind the cauldron, and hope for the best.

The giant tied up each goat by a rope to rings in the cave wall, and that took him more time than a short time, and he not seeing me. Then he came over to the cauldron, and though I was for crawling away, he saw me. So I stood up and faced him.

'Ho, Conall Yellowclaw, so it's yourself, is it?' said he. 'I've been expecting you this long time. I'm thinking your young tender flesh will be a titbit for my supper.'

'A flea-bite is all the whole of me would be to you,' said I. 'And once swallowed of no more use to you. But I see that though you have two eyes, you have only the sight of one of them. Now all the world knows that I am skilled in the art of healing. You had best keep me alive to restore the sight to your blind eye.'

'Keep you alive *until* you've restored it, I'm thinking,' said he, and gives a great stupid spluttering laugh at his own pleasantry.

'And that will be longer than you think,' said I to myself.

I made the giant lie down on his back, and I twisted up some roots and stout stems of heather into a brush. And, as if by mistake, I poked the brush into his good eye and made it as blind as the other.

'And now good-bye,' said I, and made a run for the mouth of the cave.

But he gave a leap beyond me, and stood himself in the mouth of the cave, and howled that he would have my life for the trick I had played him. He was feeling around to get at me and kill me; but I climbed up and squeezed myself into a crack of rock, and neither stirred nor sneezed, and so I was safe from him till morning.

In the morning he was for letting the goats loose, but it was too much for him to untie the ropes without his sight. So he roared for me to come and do it.

'Not I!' said I. 'You'll kill me!'

'I swear I won't kill you till it's done,' said he, and went to stand in the mouth of the cave.

I drew my dagger and I killed the billy-goat, and started to flay it.

'I think you are up to some mischief!' said the giant.

'I am not,' said I. 'But the knots are so tight it takes time to loose them.'

So then I freed one of the nanny-goats, and she trotted to the mouth of the cave, and the giant put his hands on her, and said, 'Is it thou, my pretty little white goat? Thou seest me, but I cannot see thee.'

I freed the nanny-goats slowly, one by one; and one by one they went through the mouth of the cave, and the giant felt them, and counted them, and caressed them as they passed.

And for dear life, between the freeing of one nanny-goat and the next, I was flaying the hide off the billy-goat. And when I had it off, I went down on my hands and knees, and drew the hide over me, the back over my back, the head over my head, with the long horns standing up, and the face over my face. And so, having loosed the last of the nanny-goats, I crawled in my goatskin to the mouth of the cave.

The giant laid his hands on me when I got there. 'Is it thou, my proud shaggy buck?' said he. 'Thou seest me, but I cannot see thee. And art thou come last, that should come first? Now I will kill the rascal that put this shame on thee!'

But I passed between his feet.

So, when I was out of the cave, I stood upright, and threw the goatskin from me.

'And now good-bye to you!' said I.

'Art thou got out then, Conall?' said he. 'That was a rare trick you played on me, and I am fairly beaten! Come nearer and I will give you a ring, to keep me in your memory.'

'I will not come nearer,' said I. 'But if you will throw the ring, I will pick it up.'

So he threw the ring on the sea-shore, and I picked it up and put it on my finger.

'Have you the ring?' said he.

'I have,' said I.

'And is it fitting you?' said he.

'It is,' said I.

So then he called out, 'Ring, where are you?'

And the ring answered, 'I am here.'

And he came running towards the sound.

Then I tried to pull off the ring and cast it away, but the ring clung to my finger as if it grew there. I turned and ran hither and thither over the sand and among the rocks, with the giant after me; and ever he was calling, 'Ring, where are you?' and it was answering, 'I am here.'

So when I saw that I could not get the ring off, and that there was no way of escape for me but one way, I drew my dagger and cut off the finger that had the ring on it, and threw finger and ring far out into deep water.

And the giant called again, 'Ring, where are you?'

And the ring answered out of the deep water, 'I am here.'

And the giant waded in, he ever calling and the ring ever answering, till he came to the deep water, and it closed over his head, and he was drowned.

So then I went back into the cave and collected all of the giant's treasure, and took it home to delight my parents.

That's the end of my story, says Conall Yellowclaw. And if you look at my left hand, you will see that the middle finger is missing, and that I have one of yellow gold in its place.

10 · The Brave Little Tailor

One hot summer morning, a merry little tailor sat cross-legged on his table by the open window, stitching away at a waistcoat. He had given his prentice boy a holiday, so he was alone in the workshop.

And as he sat and stitched, he heard a woman passing by in the street down below, calling out, 'Honey for sale! Fine honey for sale!'

It seemed a long time since breakfast, and the tailor thought he could do with a slice of bread and honey. So he put his head out of the window and called, 'Come up here, my good woman!'

The woman came up, and the tailor bought a very small pot of honey. The woman thought it hadn't been worth her while to come up all those stairs in the heat, and she went away grumbling. But, bless me! The tailor didn't worry about her grumbles! He cut a good slice of bread, spread the honey thickly upon it, and put it tidily on a plate beside him.

'I will just finish this seam before I eat,' said he.

And he went on stitching.

Very soon the flies smelt the honey and came buzzing into the room.

'Be off with you!' cried the tailor, flapping his handkerchief at the flies. 'Nobody invited *you* to dinner!'

But the flies had invited themselves, it seems, and they wouldn't be off with them. They buzzed up from the tailor's flapping handkerchief, and then they buzzed down again, and began crawling over the bread and honey. The tailor brought down his hand-kerchief, *smack!* Some of the flies escaped, but seven of them lay dead on the table.

'Seven at one blow!' said the tailor. 'What a clever fellow I am! The whole world ought to know about this!'

So he made himself a belt, and stitched on it the words, SEVEN AT ONE BLOW. He put on the belt, and walked out into the world. For if the world ought to know about him, the world *should* know about him.

He walked out of the town, and quite a long way farther. At last he came to the king's palace, and by now he was feeling tired. So he went into the palace gardens, stretched himself out on his back on a green, grassy lawn, and fell asleep.

Whilst he was sleeping, the king came out into the gardens, and read the words written on the belt.

'*Seven at one blow!*' said he, thinking, of course, that it was seven *men* the tailor had killed. 'What a hero! In time of war such a fellow would be very useful to me!'

And he wakened the tailor, and asked him if he would like to be made a knight and enter his service.

'It was for that purpose I came here,' said the tailor.

So the little tailor was knighted. He now rode about on a magnificent charger, and gave himself airs, and thought, 'How brave and lucky I am!'

'What a proud fellow he is!' said the other knights. 'And suppose he were to pick a quarrel with us – where should we be then?' And they all went in a body to the king, and told him they wished to leave his service. 'How can we hold our own against a man who can take seven lives at one blow?' they said.

'But I can't do without you!' said the king, greatly troubled. 'Plague take the fellow! I wish I had never set eyes on him! I'm afraid of him myself! But I daren't dismiss him, lest he turn round and kill us all – *whack, whack, whack!* – seven of us at each blow. What can I do?'

Then he thought of a plan. He sent for the tailor and asked if he would do him a favour. 'It's something I couldn't ask any one else,' said he. 'But, well, you know – *seven at one blow* – *you* won't have any difficulty. It's just that I want you to kill two giants for me.'

'Only *two*?' said the brave little tailor.

'Only two for the present,' said the king. 'But they're big and fierce ones. They've devoured so many of my people already, and killed so many of the knights I sent against them, that if you don't kill them, I really don't know what I shall do. When you *have* killed them, I'll give you the hand of my only daughter in marriage.' ('I can safely promise him that,' thought the king, 'for he won't come back alive.') 'Now will you go on this adventure? You shall have a troop of one hundred knights to support you.'

'Of course I'll go,' said the brave little tailor. 'But I don't want your hundred knights. A man who can kill seven at one blow can surely manage two!'

But the king insisted on his taking the knights. Perhaps he wanted them to come galloping back to him with news of the tailor's death.

The little tailor rode off to the wood where the giants lived, and the hundred knights rode behind him. When they came to the edge of the wood, the tailor jumped off his horse, and tied it to a tree. 'You stop here,' said he to the knights, 'whilst I go and see to the giants.'

The knights were glad enough to stay behind, and the brave little tailor skipped off by himself into the wood.

He skipped along, and he skipped along, but warily, and keeping a sharp look-out for the two giants. And in the middle of the wood he found them, asleep under a tree. He ran round for a while then, filling his pocket full of stones, and after a time he climbed into the tree.

He crept out on to a branch just over the giants' heads, and began throwing stones down on one of them. This giant woke up, and gave the other a prod.

'What did you hit me for?' he grumbled.

'Didn't hit you,' said the second giant. 'You were dreaming.'

Both the giants went to sleep again, and the tailor threw stones at the second giant. One stone fell on his ear, and another on his nose, and he woke up with a growl.

'Stop pelting me!' said he.

'Didn't pelt you,' said the first giant. 'Must have been dreaming.'

'*Wasn't* dreaming,' said the second giant. 'My nose is bleeding!'

'Can't help that,' said the first giant.

Well, they squabbled for a bit, and then they made it up, and went to sleep again. And the tailor dropped the largest stone he had, *wallop*, right on the first giant's eye.

'This is more than I can stand!' he shouted, scrambling up in a fury. 'You've blacked my eye!'

'Didn't black your eye!' roared the second giant. 'It's you that's cut my lip and broken my front teeth!' For the tailor had meanwhile dropped another large stone right into the second giant's open mouth.

It wasn't just squabbling with those two giants after that. It was a stand-up fight, and 'I'll show you, you blackguard!' and rooting up of trees to hammer each other with, and 'take that, and take that, and take *that*!' and roaring and heaving and panting and groaning, till at last they both dropped to the ground, and lay there side by side, dead as dead.

Then the little tailor skipped down from the tree, drew his

sword, hacked the dead giants here and there about the body, and went back to his hundred knights.

'The deed is done, and the giants are dead,' said he. 'It was a fierce battle. They tore up trees for their defence. But what defence is a tree against a man who can kill seven at one blow? Come and see!'

The knights followed him into the wood, and looked at the dead giants lying among the uprooted trees.

'And you haven't so much as a scratch on you!' said they in amaze.

'Pooh!' said the brave little tailor. 'There were but two of them.' And they all rode back to the palace.

The king was as vexed as could be. He didn't want to give the tailor his daughter in marriage. 'What a fool I was to promise him anything!' he thought. 'But if I don't keep my promise, perhaps he will kill me!' So he said to the tailor, 'Yes, yes, we must arrange for the wedding without delay. But there's just one easy little job I would like you to do for me first.'

And he told the tailor of a unicorn that lived in another wood. 'Just catch him and bring him along,' said the king. 'I have a fancy that a live unicorn would grace the wedding celebrations.'

Now this unicorn was the wildest and fiercest beast that ever ran on four legs, and the king felt sure that the tailor could never catch it alive. Either it would kill him, or he would come back defeated, so in any case there would be no wedding.

The tailor took a halter and an axe and went on foot into the wood to catch the unicorn. Soon he heard the sound of galloping hoofs, and there was the unicorn charging down on him with its eyes flashing, and its long, glittering horn held like a spear, ready to run him through.

'Not so fast, not so fast, my friend!' said the brave little tailor.

He waited till that long, glittering horn was within a foot of

94

him, and then he dodged behind a big tree. The unicorn was going too fast to stop itself; and the horn went into the tree, and stuck there. The creature kicked and struggled and neighed and stamped, but it couldn't pull its horn out of the tree. The tailor sat down on a bank of moss, and waited till the unicorn was tired out. Then he put the halter round its neck, and with his axe hewed away the tree from around its horn. And so led it back to the king.

'I'm delighted,' said the king, 'and we would have the wedding at once, only I've just heard of a wild boar that's doing terrible damage and killing every one it meets. I intend to give all my subjects a holiday for the wedding; but how can they enjoy a holiday with the fear of death upon them? So just go and catch the boar for me, will you? And then we can have the wedding in peace. I'll give you a hundred huntsmen to help you.'

'Hunting a wild boar is the kind of sport I enjoy,' said the brave little tailor. 'But what do I need with your hundred huntsmen?'

However, the king made him take them along.

'He'll never catch that boar,' said the king. And he went into the palace and told his daughter there would be no wedding.

As the tailor and the huntsmen went along the road, they met a crowd of people running towards them. 'The boar! The wild boar!' they were screaming and shouting.

The huntsmen took to their heels; the brave little tailor was left alone, and the huge boar was rushing at him, foaming and gnashing its tusks.

The tailor turned and ran like a streak of light; but he didn't run far. There was a chapel by the side of the way, and in through the door of the chapel he darted, and out again at the window. The wild boar charged after him into the chapel, and the tailor raced round outside and slammed the door on it. The creature was too heavy and clumsy to leap out of the window, so there it was trapped. And the brave little tailor went back to the king.

'I've caught the boar,' said he, 'and now you can do what you like with it. But first we'll have the wedding, because I'm tired of being put off.'

The king couldn't think of any more excuses, so the tailor married the princess. He was proud as a peacock, and the princess was proud, too. She thought she had got a great warrior-hero for a husband.

But one night she heard the tailor talking in his sleep. He was dreaming that he was back in the workshop, and, 'Boy,' said he, 'finish off that waistcoat, and stitch these trousers for me at once, or I'll clout you over the head with the yard-stick!'

In the morning the princess went weeping to the king. 'You've disgraced me forever,' she sobbed. 'If not a prince, I thought at least you had given me a hero for a husband. But he is only a miserable little tailor!'

The king was greatly shocked. But he thought of a plan to comfort her. 'Tonight,' said he, 'when your husband is asleep, open the door between the bedroom and the dressing-room. The dressing-room will be full of armed men. They will creep in and bind that wretched little tailor before he can waken, and we will put him in a ship, and the ship shall sail away with him to the other end of the world.'

The princess agreed. But it so happened that the brave little tailor had a faithful page; and the faithful page overheard what the king said to the princess, and off he went to tell his master.

That night, when the princess thought the tailor was asleep, she got up and softly opened the bedroom door. She peeped out and saw that the dressing-room was full of armed men, and then she went and lay down again. Immediately the tailor, who was only pretending to be asleep, began to talk.

'Boy,' said he, 'finish off that waistcoat, and stitch these trousers for me at once, or I'll clout you over the head with the yard-stick. I've killed seven at one blow, slain two giants, and caught a unicorn and a wild boar. Is it likely that I should be afraid of anyone out there in the dressing-room?'

And when the armed men, who were in the dressing-room waiting to bind the tailor, heard these words, they threw down their weapons and their strong cords, and fled. And there was not one of the king's subjects who dared to touch the brave little tailor after that.

So the king had to make the best of his son-in-law, and the princess had to make the best of her husband. There was a lot to be said for him: he was merry, and brave, and clever, and in the end she came to love him.

11 · The Giant who had no Heart in his Body

Once upon a time there was a king who had seven sons, and the time came for them to marry. So six of them set off in grand array to go a-courting. But the king, who loved all his sons very dearly, wouldn't let the youngest go; he said he must keep one son by him to gladden his eyes, and the six others between them could surely choose and bring home a bride for their youngest brother.

The six princes, with their horses and dogs and train of servants, rode till they came into a country whose king had six beautiful daughters, and the six princes and the six princesses fell in love with each other. The king was willing that his daughters should marry the princes; and so, with great rejoicings, the six princes set out on their return journey home, each with his bride riding alongside of him.

But they hadn't found a bride for their youngest brother, Halvor. They were so happy that they had forgotten all about him.

Now as they were riding along, and had ridden far, and had still far to go, they came to a high, black hill, in which lived a giant who turned people into stone with one glare of his huge eyes. And that's what happened to the six princes and the six princesses, and to their horses and their dogs and their train of servants: the giant came out and glared at them, and they were all turned into stone.

The days passed, and the princes' father became more and more anxious. 'Why don't my sons come home, why *don't* they?' he cried.

'Father, let me go and look for them,' said Halvor.

'No, no!' said the king. 'If I lose you, I shall have no sons at all!'

But Halvor kept on morning, noon, and night, saying, 'Let me go, father! Father, let me go!' till at last the king agreed, and Halvor rode away. But his brothers and their train of servants had taken all the horses but one, and that one was very old and slow; so that, though Halvor *rode* away, he would have been quicker walking.

He hadn't gone far when he saw a raven lying in the road, fluttering his wings, and unable to rise.

'Oh, dear prince,' said the raven, 'I'm starving! Pray give me some food, and in your greatest need I will come to your aid.'

'Poor bird,' said Halvor, 'I don't know that you could ever be of any help to me. But you're welcome to some of my food.'

He got off his horse, and set his bag of food down on the road. 'Help yourself!' said he.

And the raven ate the lot, and flew away.

Prince Halvor rode on till he came to a stream, and on the bank he saw a salmon, flapping and gasping.

'Oh, dear prince,' gasped the salmon, 'lift me up and put me in the water, and in your utmost need I'll come to your aid.'

Halvor lifted the salmon gently, and put her back in the stream. 'But I don't see how *you* are going to help me!' said he.

And the salmon swam away.

He hadn't gone much farther when his poor old horse dropped dead under him. So he left it at the side of the road and walked on.

And what should he meet next but a starving wolf. The wolf

was so weak that he couldn't stand on his legs, but was crawling along the road on his belly.

'Oh, dear prince,' said the wolf, 'pray, *pray* give me some food, and in your great need I will come to your aid.'

'I haven't any food,' said Halvor, 'I met a hungry raven, and he ate it all. What can I do for you?' Then he remembered his horse. 'My horse is lying dead by the roadside,' said he. 'Could you make a meal of that?'

The wolf crawled away and ate the horse, and then his strength returned to him, and he came galloping after Halvor. 'Get on my back, dear prince,' said he, 'and tell me where you want to go.'

'I am looking for my six brothers,' said Halvor.

So the wolf said they had been turned into stone, and he would show Halvor where they were. And away they went, faster than the wind blows, over down and dale till they came to the giant's hill. And there, outside the hill, stood a multitude of stone figures — the six princes, and the six princesses, and their horses and their dogs and their long train of servants.

There was a door in the black hill behind the stone figures.

'You must go in through that door,' said the wolf, 'for that is where the giant lives.'

'But what is the use of *my* being turned into stone as well?' said Halvor.

The wolf glared at him quite angrily. 'Are you a coward?' said he. 'Do as I say!'

So then Halvor opened the door and went in, though he didn't half like the idea.

He walked through a lot of empty rooms, and in the last room he found a princess sitting; and she was as beautiful as the sun on a spring morning.

'Oh why have you come?' said she. 'Oh please go away, before it is too late! You may be brave and think you will kill the giant, but no one can kill him, for he has no heart in his body!'

'But I must try and free my brothers,' said Halvor. 'And I must free you, too,' said he. For he was feeling quite bold and reckless at the sight of her. 'No, I won't go away, say what you will!'

So then the princess sprinkled some of her scent over him, so that the giant shouldn't smell him. And she told him to creep under the bed; and she fetched some of her robes and heaped them over him, to hide him.

Soon after that, the giant came in, and the princess sang for him, and danced for him, to put him in a good temper. And she *did* put him in a good temper. So, said he, 'Now, sweetheart, what shall I give you for singing and dancing so prettily?'

'You have already given me everything I want,' said the princess. 'But there is just one question I should like to ask you – if I dared.'

'Ask away,' said he, stroking her golden hair with his ugly great hand.

'Where do you keep your heart?' said the princess, 'since it's not in your body?'

'Ho!' said the giant. 'Under the door-sill.'

Next morning, as soon as the giant had gone out, Halvor and the princess got a pickaxe, and dragged up the door-sill. They dug under it and dug under it, but they couldn't find the heart. So they put back the door-sill and made all tidy. But they were bitterly disappointed.

'I must try him again,' said the princess. And she went out and picked armfuls of flowers, and arranged them in beautiful nosegays all round the door-sill.

Then she sprinkled Halvor with some more of her scent, told him to hide under the bed, and covered him up with her robes.

When the giant came in, he stared at the nosegays.

'Who put these here?' said he.

'I did,' said the princess.

'What for?' said the giant.

'To show my love,' said the princess. 'Because your heart lies there.'

'Ho, you silly little bit of summer sunshine!' said the giant, pinching her cheek with his ugly great fingers. 'But it don't lie there.'

'Then where does it lie?' said the princess.

'In yonder cupboard against the wall,' said the giant. And he laughed a great laugh.

In the morning, as soon as the giant had gone out, Halvor and the princess were at that cupboard in a twinkling. It was full of lumber of every kind. The mice ran out of it squeaking, and fat hairy spiders dropped on their heads and hands; but they didn't stop their search for that. They turned everything out, and then put everything back. For the giant's heart was not there.

'I could sit down and cry!' said the princess.

But she didn't sit down and cry. She went out and gathered armfuls of flowers; and she and Halvor made them into garlands, and they hung the garlands on the cupboard.

Then she sprinkled Halvor with her scent yet a third time, and he hid under the bed, and she flung her robes over him.

'What's the meaning of all this foolishness?' said the giant, when he came in and saw the garlands.

'Oh, *don't* call it foolishness!' cried the princess. 'How could I help but deck the place where your heart lies hidden?'

'And suppose it don't lie hidden there?' said the giant.

'Then where *does* it lie hidden?' said she.

'That's my secret,' said he.

And would he tell her? No, he wouldn't.

So then the princess put on her finest clothes, and made herself look as pretty as ever she could, and set herself to amuse the giant.

She danced for him, and she sang for him, and played all his favourite tunes on the harp, and petted and praised him, till the silly old giant was quite beside himself with delight, and told her she might ask for anything she wished.

'Then tell me truly this time,' said she. 'Where *do* you keep your heart?'

'Where you will never come, my precious,' said he.

'I don't want to come there,' said she. 'I only want to know.'

'Why for?' said he.

'So's I can lie and dream of it,' said she. 'For what sweeter dream could I wish than that?'

'Ho, you lovely, wicked little witch!' said he. 'How can I refuse you anything? But swear to me first that the secret shall never pass your lips.'

'I swear,' said she.

So then he told her.

'Over yonder lies a lake, and in that lake there lies an island; on that island stands a church, and in that church there is a well; in that well there swims a duck; in that duck there is an egg; and in that egg lies my heart. . . . And now, sweet dreams to you!'

In the morning, when the giant had gone out, Halvor crept from under the bed, and the princess said to him, 'Now you must do what you can. I can help you no further.'

'I must go to the well in the church,' said Halvor. 'If only I knew where "over yonder" was!'

He opened the door of the giant's hill, and there was the wolf waiting for him.

'Jump on my back,' said the wolf. 'I'll take you "over yonder".'

So Halvor jumped on the wolf's back, and away they went, faster than the wind blows, over dale and down, from here to yonder. When they got to the lake, the wolf jumped in and swam, and never stopped till they came to the island.

104

On the island stood a church. But the church door was locked, and the key of the door hung in a tower high out of reach.

'Call on the raven,' said the wolf.

So prince Halvor called on the raven, and the raven came, and fetched the key out of the tower and gave it to Halvor. And Halvor unlocked the church door and went in.

In the church there was a well, and on the well there swam a duck; and the prince coaxed the duck with bread till it came to the well-side, and then he made a grab at it. But, just as he was lifting the duck from the water, it dropped the egg, and the egg sank to the bottom of the well.

'Call on the salmon,' said the wolf.

So prince Halvor called on the salmon, and the salmon came, and she fetched the egg from the bottom of the well, and gave it to the prince.

'Now give the egg a squeeze,' said the wolf.

The prince gave the egg a squeeze, and far away they heard the giant screaming.

'Squeeze harder,' said the wolf.

Halvor squeezed harder, and far away they heard the giant's screaming voice begging that Halvor would spare his life.

'Tell him you will spare his life if he will give you back your six brothers and their six brides, and their horses and their dogs and all their retainers,' said the wolf.

So Halvor told the giant that. And very soon the giant's voice came screaming that all the stone figures were restored to life, and waiting for Halvor.

'Now,' said the wolf, 'break the egg in two.'

'Nay,' said prince Halvor. 'After my promise that would be mean!'

'Mean!' snarled the wolf. '*Mean?* Now you have your brothers back, are you going to let the giant live to turn other folk to stone? Here! Give me the egg!'

He snatched it in his jaws, and bit it in two. And the giant burst with a bang.

Then Halvor went back to the giant's hill, and found his brothers and their brides and their dogs and their horses and their retainers alive and merry. And he went in through the door in the hill, and took the princess by the hand, and said, 'Here is *my* bride!'

The wolf took Halvor and the princess on his back, and the whole company rode home.

The king their father wept for joy when his seven sons came home to him, each with his bride. There was a grand wedding ceremony, and a grand feast. The wolf and the raven came to the wedding; and the salmon, also, had an invitation, which pleased her very much, although she had to decline it.

12· The Three Golden Hairs of the King of the Cave Giants

Once upon a time a poor woodcutter lived with his wife on the edge of a forest. For a while, there were only the two of them, and then the wife had a baby boy. One stormy night the woodcutter looked at the baby in the cradle and said, 'Wife, I would like my boy to do better in the world than I have done.'

No sooner had he said that, than there came a knock at the door.

The woodcutter hastened to open the door, and there in the wind and the rain stood a lean man, with the water dripping off the cloak that he wore.

'Come in out of the storm and dry yourself,' said the woodcutter. And the lean man stepped inside, hung up his wet cloak on a peg, and sat down beside the hearth.

Now the wife had nothing in the house for supper but four sausages and some black bread. But when she saw how their visitor shivered and shook with the cold, and how lean he was, she served him up all four sausages, whilst she and the woodcutter ate only dry bread. And if the lean man noticed that, he didn't say a word.

It was the same when bedtime came. There was only one bed in the cottage, and the lean man had it, whilst the woodcutter and his wife lay on the floor. And if the lean man noticed *that*, he didn't say a word.

Before daybreak, the woodcutter took his gun and went into the forest and shot a hare. The wife cooked it for breakfast. The lean man ate three-quarters of it, and the woodcutter and his wife had only one quarter between them. Then the lean man got up to go.

'Filled, rested, and dried,' said he, 'and nothing to give you in return.'

'We are not looking for a return,' said the woodcutter.

'But I have, at any rate, something to tell you,' said the lean man. 'Your little son will grow up to marry the king's daughter.'

And he was on with his cloak and out through the door, before the woodcutter and his wife could recover from their surprise.

How the news got about, no one could say; but it wasn't many days before every one in the near-by village knew what the lean man had foretold for the woodcutter's baby. The news spread from the village to the palace, and soon the king heard of it, and he fell into a rage.

'Marry my daughter!' said he. 'A woodcutter's brat! We'll soon put a stop to that nonsense!'

So off he rode to the woodcutter's cottage pretending to have lost his way out hunting. He stooped over the baby in its little wooden cradle, and said it was the loveliest child he had ever set eyes on. 'You must let me take him to the palace, and rear him as a companion for my daughter,' said he.

The mother wasn't willing, but the woodcutter whispered, 'There's fate in this, wife. Remember the words of the lean man!'

So then the mother wrapped the baby in a warm shawl, and the king took it, cradle and all, and set it before him on his horse, and galloped away with it. He galloped till he came to a deep, swift-flowing stream, and into that stream he flung the baby in its cradle.

'Be off with you to the bottom,' said he, 'and marry the daughter of a fish! You won't get *my* daughter!' And away he galloped.

But he hadn't thought to put a stone in the cradle along with the baby, so the cradle didn't sink. The stream carried it on till it came to the miller's dam, and there the miller saw it, and drew it ashore.

He carried the baby into the mill. 'Wife,' said he, 'we have often mourned that we have no children. Now see what the stream has brought us!'

So the miller and his wife brought up the baby, and loved him as their own son. They called him Peterlin, because the *lin*, or stream, had brought him. And he grew so handsome and strong and proud and fearless you would have said he was a prince in disguise, to look at him, and not the son of a poor woodcutter.

Now when Peterlin was eighteen and was working one day

outside the mill, who should come riding by but the king and his train of courtiers. When the king saw Peterlin, he was astonished at his beauty, and thought he would like him as a page. So he sent for the miller.

'That's a handsome lad, that son of yours,' said the king to the miller.

'Handsome, truly, sire,' said the miller. 'But not my son, an't please you.' And he told the king how he had found Peterlin in the mill-dam.

Then the king knew who the lad was. And did he want him for a page after that? No, he did *not*! But he smiled a false crooked smile, and said he, 'My lady queen has gone on a visit to one of my northern castles, and I wish to send her a letter. Will you allow this fine lad to carry it for me? I know he can be trusted, and the queen delights in beauty.'

The miller was willing. The king wrote a letter and sealed it, and Peterlin set out on his journey, pleased that the king should so single him out and favour him. But he wouldn't have been so pleased could he have read the message inside that sealed letter, for it told the queen to have the bearer beheaded immediately.

Peterlin walked northward all day, but when night came he lost his way in a wood where wolves were howling. So, seeing a light in a large hut, he knocked, and asked for a night's lodging.

The woman who opened the door looked on him pityingly. 'Poor pretty lad,' said she, 'you don't know what you ask! This is a robbers' den. If, when the robbers return, they find you here, they will strip you naked.'

'I have nothing on me worth stealing,' said Peterlin. 'The robbers are men, like myself. I would rather spend the night with them than with the wolves out there in the wood.'

So then the woman took him in, and put him to sleep in a little back room. She covered him up with a wolf skin, and told him to lie very quiet, and then perhaps the robbers would not notice him.

But the robbers did notice him; it wasn't much they they missed!

Peterlin was sound asleep. The robber chief crept in to him very quietly, to see if he had anything on him worth stealing. He felt in Peterlin's pockets and found the king's letter, took it out, broke the seal, and read it under the kitchen lamp.

Now the robber chief and the king were at odds, as well they might be; for the king was always threatening to hang the robbers, if only he could catch them. So when the robber chief read the letter, he grinned a great grin, and called for a pen, took paper and wrote another letter and sealed it in the same manner, and put this new letter into Peterlin's pocket without waking him.

And this is what the new letter said: 'Marry the bearer to our daughter immediately.'

Well, the queen was a bit surprised when Peterlin arrived and she read that letter. But a queen must do what the king tells her; and, moreover, she was greatly taken with Peterlin's beauty. As for the princess, she fell in love with Peterlin the moment she saw him, and he fell in love with her. So they were married that day, and the lean man's words came true.

The wedding festivities lasted for three days; and they were all still feasting and rejoicing when the king arrived.

'What is the meaning of this?' said he, white with rage.

'I did as your majesty commanded,' said the queen, and she showed him the letter.

The king had to pretend pleasure, and he smiled crooked smiles, but he raged in his false wicked heart. 'The rascal may have married my daughter,' thought he, 'but I'll outwit him yet!'

So he called Peterlin to him, and said, 'Now that you are a prince, you must prove your mettle.'

'Willingly,' said Peterlin, 'if you will but tell me how.'

'Bring me three golden hairs from the head of the king of the Cave Giants,' said the king. 'If you succeed in doing that, I shall know you are worthy to rule over my kingdom when I am dead.'

'But he won't succeed,' thought the king. 'The giant will kill him.' And he laughed in his false, wicked heart.

Peterlin kissed the princess good-bye, and set out. After walking a long way, he came to a city, and asked the guards at the gate to let him through.

'Who are you?' said one of the guards. 'What are you doing? And what do you know?'

'I am Prince Peterlin,' said he. 'I am walking on my way. And I know everything.'

'Then can you tell us,' said the guard, 'why it is that the fountain in our market-place has dried up? The reward for answering that question is two asses laden with gold.'

'I will tell you when I come back,' said Peterlin.

And the guards let him through.

After a while he came to another city, and asked the guards at the gate to let him through.

'Who are you?' said they. 'What are you doing? And what do you know?'

'I am Prince Peterlin,' said he. 'I am walking on my way. And I know everything.'

Then the guards asked him why the apple tree that grew in the city park, and used to bear golden apples, did not now bear even leaves. If he could answer that question, he would get four asses laden with gold.

'I will tell you when I come back,' said Peterlin.

And the guards let him through.

Late in the afternoon he came to a lake, and called to the ferryman to row him across. The ferryman asked who he was, what he

was doing, and what he knew. And Peterlin again said that he
knew everything.

'Then tell me,' said the ferryman, 'why it is that I must forever
row people forth and back over this lake, and can never get away
from my boat. If you can answer that question, I will give you
eight asses laden with gold.'

'I will tell you when I come back,' said Peterlin.

And the ferryman rowed him across the lake.

And so, in the end, he came to where the king of the Cave Giants
lived, in a gloomy cavern as broad as a mountain.

The giant himself was not at home, but the giant's grandmother was sitting outside the cave in a rocking-chair, twiddling
her great thumbs.

'Go away, my handsome, pretty boy,' said she.

'I can't go away,' said Peterlin, 'until I have three of the giant's
golden hairs.'

'How's that then?' said she.

'Because if I don't get them, the king will kill me,' said Peterlin.

'Kill 'ee?' said she. 'And you such a handsome pretty boy! Nay,
nay, the king shan't kill 'ee. Grandma'll help 'ee get the golden
hairs.'

'And I should like to know the answer to three questions,' said
Peterlin. And he told her about the fountain, and the apple tree,
and the ferryman.

'My lor!' said she, 'ain't you a troublesome child! But you're a
pretty one! Grandma'll see what she can do for 'ee.'

And she changed Peterlin into an ant.

She had just hidden him in a fold of her skirt when the giant
came home. And if she was big, he was bigger, and cast his shadow
over the whole country.

'Fee! Fi! Foh! Fum! I smell the blood—' he began.

But she took him up short.

113

'There you go again, with your *fee, fi, fumming!*' said she. 'If there be a man, find him. And if there baint no man, don't stand there snuffing, but pick up my chair and carry it in for me, and we'll sit us down to supper.'

The giant couldn't find a man, so he carried the chair into the cave, and his grandmother gave him a good supper. And after supper, she sat in her rocking-chair, and the giant laid his head in her lap, and she stroked his golden hair for him, and he fell asleep.

Soon as he was snoring, she tweaked a hair out of his head.

'What you doing of?' he cried, waking up very cross.

'Save us!' said she. 'I must have grabbed a hold of your head in my sleep, I was that frightened! I dreamed I was shut up in a strange city, and the guards wouldn't let me out till I told 'em why their fountain had gone dry. But how could I tell 'em, when I didn't know?'

'Then if you dream that dream again,' said the giant, 'you can tell 'em from me that there's a toad squatting under a stone at the foot of the fountain. Kill the toad and the fountain flows again. Now, leave me sleep in peace.'

Soon as he was asleep snoring, the grandmother pulled out another hair, and he woke with a bellow.

'You're at it again, are 'ee? What do 'ee want? What's the matter with 'ee?'

'Oh,' said she, 'I clutched at your head in my dream, I was that frighted! I dreamed I was in another strange city, and the guards were going to kill me, because I couldn't tell them why their apple tree, that used to bear golden apples, don't now bear even a leaf. How could I tell 'em, when I don't know?'

'Well, you can tell 'em from me,' said the giant, 'that there's a mouse gnawing at the roots. Catch the mouse and the tree will bear golden apples again. *Now* will you leave me sleep in peace?'

'Well sleep then,' said she. '*I'm* not hindering of 'ee!'

So the giant slept and snored. The grandmother pulled out the third golden hair, and he woke raging.

The grandmother said she'd dreamed that the ferryman was killing her, because she couldn't tell him why he could never get out of his boat.

'Tell him from me,' said the giant, 'that if he puts the rudder into the hand of a passenger, he will be free, and the passenger must take his place. Now I'll sleep. And if you wake me again, *I'll kill 'ee myself!'*

'Shan't wake you again,' said the grandmother. 'Shan't dream no more.'

And they slept. The grandmother slept in her rocking-chair, the giant slept with his head in her lap, and the little ant, that was Peterlin, slept in a fold of her skirt.

In the morning, when the giant had eaten his breakfast and gone out, the grandmother changed Peterlin back into his proper shape, and gave him the three golden hairs.

'And was you hearkening like a fox to them questions and answers?' said she.

'I was,' said Peterlin.

'Oh ho! Grandma's the one to help a sweet pretty boy!' she chuckled. And she gave him a smacking kiss that fair knocked him backward.

So, with his three golden hairs, Peterlin set out on his way back. When he came to the lake, the ferryman said, 'Now Master-Know-It-All, tell me the answer to my question.'

'You have only to put the rudder into the hand of your passenger, and you will be free, and he will have to take your place,' said Peterlin.

'As simple as that!' said the delighted ferryman.

'As simple as that,' said Peterlin.

'The eight asses laden with gold are tied up under yonder tree,' said the ferryman. 'Bring them along, and I'll ferry the lot of you over.'

But Peterlin drove the asses round the lake, lest the ferryman should put the rudder into *his* hand.

By and by he came to the city where the apple tree grew, and the guards asked him if he had the answer to their question.

'Yes, I have,' said Peterlin. 'At the root of the apple tree a mouse is gnawing. Catch the mouse, and the tree will bear golden apples again.'

'As simple as that!' said the guards.

'As simple as that,' said Peterlin.

So the guards dug around the roots of the tree, and caught the mouse, and immediately the tree clothed itself in brilliant green leaves and golden apples. They gave Peterlin four asses laden with gold, as they had promised.

So Peterlin came to the next city. And the guards asked him, 'Can you now tell us why our fountain is dry?'

'Yes, I can,' said Peterlin. And he told them about the toad.

'As simple as that!' said they.

'As simple as that,' said Peterlin.

So the guards dug up the stone at the foot of the fountain and found the toad, and killed it. And immediately the fountain threw up jet after jet of sparkling water. And they gave Peterlin the two asses laden with gold, as they had promised.

Now he had fourteen asses laden with gold; and driving them before him, he arrived at the palace, and gave the king the three golden hairs from the giant's head.

The false, wicked king pretended to be overjoyed to see Peterlin. 'But, dear son,' said he, 'where did you get all that gold?'

'I got the most of it by the side of the lake,' said Peterlin.

'The near side, or the far side?' said the king.

'The far side,' said Peterlin.

So the bad, greedy king set out at once for the lake, to get some gold-laden asses for himself. When he got to the lake, he shouted to the ferryman to row him across. The ferryman brought the boat in, thrust the rudder into the king's hands, and leaped ashore.

'What is the meaning of this?' said the king.

'You'll soon find out,' said the ferryman. And off he went, laughing.

So there was the false wicked king, stuck in that boat, and rowing forth and back, forth and back over the lake till doomsday. And there was Peterlin king in his stead.

The woodcutter and his wife came to live at the palace; and Peterlin sent his fourteen asses laden with gold to the miller and his wife. And there were great rejoicings.

13. Prince Loaf

Once upon a time there was an orphan boy who looked after the king's sheep. He slept where he could, and ate what he could, and his bed was hard and his food scanty. Nobody thought anything of him at all, except the king's young daughter, who had the kindest heart in the world. And she, when she walked in her father's fields, and passed the place where the shepherd boy was, would smile and say, 'How are the sheep today, shepherd?'

'All is well with them, your royal highness,' he would answer. And that is all he ever said to her. But she was to him as the morning star that wakes the singing birds before the dawn, and he loved her dearly.

Now one summer evening, when he was lying on the grass beside the sheep, thinking to sleep there, as the night was warm, he heard the sound of someone crying. It was a very big sound, and a very mournful one, like the wind sobbing among forest trees; but it was certainly someone crying. Almost the boy thought he could hear the tears falling. So he got up and searched about, and the sound of crying led him to the edge of a forest. And there, under a tree, lay a giant, with the tears rolling down his face.

The boy was very frightened, and started to run away.

But the giant called after him, '*Don't* run away! I won't hurt you. But I am in such terrible pain from a wound in my foot. I can't walk, I can't even stand, and if you won't help me, I must lie here and die.'

The boy thought it was rather babyish of the giant to cry like that; but he remembered having heard that giants have childish minds. So he came back and looked at the giant's foot, which was two yards long. And there, stuck in the underside of it, was the broken off head of a pitchfork.

'No wonder you couldn't walk!' said he. And he pulled the pitchfork out of the giant's foot, and fetched water in his drinking can, and washed away the blood, and took off his shirt, and bound up the foot.

'See if you can walk now,' said he.

The giant got up and found he could walk, though a bit lamely. And he grinned all over his kind, stupid face, and said, 'Come with me, and I will reward you. The giants are having a feast to-night, and I was on my way there. Oh, you shall see some fun, I can promise you! Though, of course, my brothers might take it into their heads to eat you.'

'Then I won't come,' said the boy.

'Stop a bit,' said the giant, 'stop a bit! Let me think! I know, I'll make you invisible! Here, take this little belt and put it round your waist.'

The boy took the belt, and put it round his waist, and he became invisible. He couldn't even see his own hands and feet.

'Are you there, boy?' said the giant.

'I'm here,' said the boy.

'Then follow me,' said the giant. And he led the boy to a clearing in the forest that was all lit up with coloured lamps, and had a fountain in the middle of it, throwing up jets of coloured water. And round about the fountain hundreds of giants and giantesses, with paper caps on their heads, were dancing and singing, and playing *Ring-a-roses* and *Nuts in May*, and other such games.

The boy had to keep a sharp look-out, not to be trodden under their great feet. The wounded giant couldn't dance, nor yet

play *Nuts in May*, so he stood on one side, and watched and giggled. And every now and then he whispered, 'Are you there, boy?'

And the boy answered, 'Yes, I'm here.'

'Keep near me,' whispered the giant after a bit. 'Something's going to happen.'

And what happened was that one of the giants tore up a weed by the roots, and under the weed was a small hole going down into the earth. Then all the giants and giantesses turned themselves into wisps of smoke, and sank, one after another, down into the hole.

'Are you there, boy?' said the last wisp of smoke, which was the wounded giant.

'Yes, I'm here,' said the boy.

'Then touch me,' said the wisp of smoke.

The boy put out his hand and touched the smoke, and sank with it down the hole into the earth.

He was seeing things that he didn't usually see, was that shepherd boy! Now he was in a great hall, and the walls of it were of gold, and so was the ceiling. And down the middle of the hall was a long table, and that was gold, too.

The table was spread for a feast, and the giants and giantesses sat round and ate like children at a Christmas party. The boy, in his invisible belt, stood on the wounded giant's knee, and reached up and helped himself; and never in his life had he eaten so much. When he could eat no more, he saw a crusty roll on the table near him; it was a tiny little roll to the giants, but a big loaf to the boy.

'Why shouldn't I take that loaf?' thought he. 'I shall be thankful to have something to eat tomorrow.'

So he took the loaf off the table.

By this time the giants and giantesses had eaten up everything. They licked up the sweet crumbs from their plates, and they sucked their sticky fingers, and they turned their gold cups upside down over their noses, to get at the last drops of the wine. They had no manners at all. And when there was left neither crumb nor drop, they began turning into wisps of smoke again, and drifting one after another up through the hole in the earth.

'Are you there, boy?' said the last wisp of smoke, that was the wounded giant.

'Yes, I'm here,' said the boy.

'Then touch me, that I may take you up with me,' said the wisp of smoke.

The boy put out his hand and touched the wisp of smoke, and there he was, standing on the earth again, with the loaf under his arm. But the giant was nowhere to be seen. So the boy went back to his sheep. He put the invisible belt and the loaf of bread into a wallet that he had left lying on the grass, and he took the wallet for his pillow, and stretched himself out, and slept soundly.

When he woke in the morning, he said to himself, 'Today I shall have some breakfast.' And he took the loaf out of his wallet, and cut at it with his knife. But, try as he would, he couldn't cut a single slice off that loaf. He was so disappointed that he felt like crying.

'I *will* have some breakfast, I *will*!' said he, and he bit at the loaf with all his might.

Crack. He thought he had broken a tooth. But when he spat out what he thought was a tooth, he found it was a gold coin. He bit at the loaf again and again, and – *crack!* – every time he bit there was a gold coin in his mouth. But the loaf remained whole.

'This is the best loaf of bread ever I had in my life!' said he, jumping to his feet. 'I shall never go hungry again!'

He put on his invisible belt, and ran to the nearest town, and went into a pie shop. There he helped himself to a good breakfast, laid down a gold coin in payment, and went back to his sheep.

In the pie shop he had heard two cooks, who were brothers, talking together. One was the king's head cook, and the other was the owner of the pie shop. The king's cook was telling his brother about a fine iced cake he was making for the princess, whose birthday it was next day.

'How *I* would like to give her something!' thought the shepherd boy.

'Well, but I can give her something!' he thought next.

He got a sack, and bit into his loaf till he had a pile of gold coins. And he filled the sack with them. And that night he put on his invisible belt, and went to the room where the princess was sleeping, and laid the sack of gold down beside the bed.

And this he did for seven nights.

The king and the queen and the princess were delighted. They thought a good fairy must be bringing the princess the sacks of gold.

'You *are* a lucky girl!' said the king.

'But oughtn't we to thank the good fairy?' said the queen.

'I don't think fairies like being thanked – or watched,' said the princess.

'No, no, of course they don't!' said the king.

But the king was very inquisitive; he had never seen a fairy, and now was his chance. So, without saying anything to the queen or the princess, he decided on the next night to hide behind a curtain in the princess' bedroom, and watch.

That night the rain was pelting down, and the wind was howling. The boy took shelter in a ruined hut to wait till it was time to go with his sack of gold to the princess' bedside. In the middle of the night, when he thought every one would be asleep, he took up the sack of gold, and ran through the wind and the rain to the palace. But, when he got there, he found he had left his invisible belt behind. He was already wet through, and he didn't want to go back through the rain to fetch it.

'Never mind,' thought he, 'no one will see me; they'll all be asleep.'

So he got in through a little window in a pantry, tiptoed up to the princess' bedroom, and opened the door without a sound. He had just put down the sack of gold by the bed, and was about to tiptoe out again, when a lamp flashed in his face, and someone seized him roughly by the arm.

'Ah, you thief!' cried the king. 'So you were going to steal the gold the good fairy brings, were you?'

The poor boy was so astonished and frightened that he couldn't get out a single word. He just stood there and trembled, and heard the king say he would throw him into a dungeon that very night. The king spoke so loudly and roughly that he woke the princess, and when she heard about the dungeon, she got out of bed and fell on her knees, and begged and prayed her father to do no such cruel thing.

'Very well,' said the king at last. 'I won't throw him into a dungeon. I will remember, instead, that he has served me faithfully up to now. But get out of my sight,' said he to the boy. 'And if ever I see your face again, I will have you hanged!'

The boy went away very sadly. He crept into the ruined hut, and sat there, wet and shivering, till morning. Then he looked at his invisible belt and his loaf, and took heart.

'I know what I'll do!' said he.

So he bit into the loaf till he had a pocketful of money. Then he walked to the nearest town and bought himself a decent suit of clothes and an old horse. And, after that, he rode off to another town.

And there, having made himself invisible, and bitten into his loaf till his pockets bulged with money, he took off the belt, and had himself fitted with a much better suit, and bought a much better horse. And in this much better suit, he rode off on his much better horse to yet a third town, and put up at the best inn, and summoned a tailor, and had a suit of clothes made fit for a prince.

Now he called himself Prince Loaf, and he walked about the town looking so grand, that though the people thought it was a funny name, they knew he must be a prince from his gracious manners, and from the way he handed money about to any one who asked for it. So he had a splendid coach made specially for him, and bought a team of magnificent horses, and hired a coachman and footmen and put them in smart livery. And then, in all this fine array, he drove off to the king's palace.

The news of Prince Loaf's coming went before him, for every one was talking about him. The king received him as an honoured guest, though he had no idea who his guest really was. But the princess recognized her little shepherd boy immediately. He told her about the giant and the belt and the loaf, and as they found they were in love with each other, they were very soon married.

The giants' loaf supplied them with all the gold they needed, and sometimes they amused themselves by putting on the invisible belt and playing hide and seek. They never stopped loving each other, so they lived happily ever after.

And that's all.